The Guardians of Iceland and other Icelandic Folk Tales

Heidi Herman

Illustrated by Michael Di Gesu

This is a work of fiction. All characters, organizations, and events portrayed in this novel are products of the author's imagination and are used fictiously.

First Edition.

Illustrations and Cover Art by Michael Di Gesu

ISBN: 0998281603
ISBN-13: 978-0998281605

DEDICATION

This book is dedicated to a group of amazing individuals that have come into or through my life. Together and separately they served as my muse and inspiration, or have provided encouragement, whether intentional or accidental. My sincerest thanks to each of you: Gretchen, Mike, Teresa, Vik, Serenity, and, of course, Mom.

Even the smallest words of encouragement can provide endless motivation. Like the lessons of a fairy tale, they can be applied over and over and are just as powerful the hundredth-time over as the first.

CONTENTS

PREFACE

Much of a culture is revealed in the legends, folklore and fairy tales that are told to children. The stories unconsciously shape the outlook, fears, and attitudes of the young. As I researched and assembled the stories for this collection, I was drawn to them for the unique insight they provided. Many of these stories have their origins in the Icelandic Sagas and from early in the settlement days. In Iceland, they often refer to them as "former days". They were shared by storytellers and few were written down in their entirety.

Icelanders rarely refer to these as "fairy tales" but rather "legends" or "folk tales". Some may have has an origins in a true story that has since been embellished and has become a legend. Many provided lessons for treatment of neighbors and fellow humans (or trolls). Lessons of tolerance, presented in "Drangey Consecrated" or an act of compassion as shown in "Hallgerður" are common themes in Icelandic folk tales. The dangers inherent in a country of waterfalls, volcanos, and sea cliffs explain the need for dire warnings of trolls and mischievous Hidden People. Children learned at an early age to be wary, not of the landscape so much as the trolls and monsters that lurked in their midst. They also learned the importance of a strong work ethic and common sense. In a country where life was difficult these were important qualities.

Over time, there have been several works that recorded these stories and many of the versions are still available today. Jón Gudmundsson the Learned (1574-1658), Árni Magnússon (1663-1730), and Jón Árnason (1819-1888) all worked to collect and record these tales. Jón Árnason is the most recognized name associated with Icelandic Folk Tales. Half of the stories included in this collection can be found in an original version in Árnason's *Icelandic Folk and Fairy Tales*. The remainder were compiled from numerous written sources, oral retelling from friends and family, and elements embedded in other stories.

The legends and folk tales had not been modernized or updated in several hundred years. In some cases, the beginning or end of the story was lost. Some appeared to wander as if two different stories were cobbled accidently along the way in history.

In this collection, I have endeavored to update the storylines to appeal to modern readers, but keep the essence and tone of the stories as close to the original as possible. I have changed the stories for readability, giving names

i

to characters, adding to the story for action, and in some cases, removing confusing elements.   The Icelandic alphabet contains some letters not found in English and the pronunciation of Icelandic words can be difficult. To assist with the readability, I have provided a phonetic approximation of the Icelandic names, to make them more manageable for children to sound out. I worked with a native Icelander to find suitable English sounds for a close pronunciation, but not all are linguistically accurate. The language did present some challenges, but I wanted to introduce as much of the culture and language as I felt possible. A pronunciation guide is also provided at the end of the book.

It was difficult to decide which stories to include because it meant excluding some from the collection.   I have grown to love all of these stories and have so enjoyed working to bring them to a larger audience.

I hope that you enjoy them as much as I do.

THE GUARDIANS OF ICELAND

Once there was a ruler named Harald Bluetooth who was King over all of Denmark and Norway, and he wanted to expand his kingdom. He decided to take over Iceland and add that to his empire. He schemed and planned, trying to find out all he could about the weaknesses of the country.

King Harald had heard wild stories about the fierce Viking warriors of Iceland. He also heard about this strange land filled with trolls, hidden folk and magical creatures. The whole land was protected by the spirits of nature. He knew he couldn't send his troops in on ships or they would be defeated quickly.

He needed to find a sneaky way to invade and take over the land. To form a plan, King Harald needed the kind of information only the very best spy could get. So, he called upon his most powerful wizard to go scout for him.

The wizard transformed himself into a whale and swam west from Denmark to the coast of Iceland. The country ahead of him was an island, almost completely round, with lots of fjords, inlets and natural bays. The wizard slowly approached the coast on the east side and looked around for just the right place to come ashore. He swam into a wide bay called Vopnafjörður (wop-na-fyore-thur) and decided it looked like a pretty good spot. But just as he neared the shore and began to concentrate on magically changing back into his human form, he heard a strange buzzing growing louder and louder.

He looked over to the mountains and saw a huge dragon come racing over the top of one and fly down through the valley directly towards him! Following close behind the dragon were hundreds of snakes and lizards squirming and slithering all over the place. They were getting closer and closer, moving quickly and spitting venom at him.

With a heaving splash of his powerful tail, the wizard quickly dove back deep in the water and swam as fast as he could back out to the sea. When he felt he was a safe distance away he stopped and looked back to the island. The massive dragon stood on the shore, raised to his full height, and spewing fire into the air. He could smell the smoky charred scent clear out in the ocean where he watched. Lined up on either side of the dragon were the lizards and lined up beside them were huge snakes. Not just any snakes, but huge, writhing, ugly sea serpents that fishermen whispered stories to one another about. He shook his big whale head and thought, *This is no place to sneak ashore!* And he swam away to the north.

As he reached the tip of the island, the wizard turned left and swam in his whale body for several hours along the northern shores. Here, he found several nice big inlets. This was much better, he thought to himself, as he made his way to a small harbor to change into his human form. No sooner had he touched his first toe on the land than he heard a terrible racket.

As he looked up, he saw a giant eagle. It was so big that as it flew, the tips of its wings touched the mountains on either side of the valley. In a flock surrounding the eagle, hundreds of birds of every kind flew towards him. They screeched and cawed, screaming at him as they dove at him. The wizard quickly jumped back into the ocean, narrowly escaping the sharp talons and beaks. He dove deep and swam away from the land as fast as he could. He swam away from the huge eagle and away from the dragon, heading further west.

He came to the western edge of the island and turned south. There, he found a large bay called Breiðafjörður (bray-the-fyore thur). He thought this looked like a good safe place to come ashore and look around. No sooner had he started to swim into the bay when he heard a loud snort. As he looked up, a large bull came towards him there, waded into the sea and began to bellow menacingly. Shimmering and swooping around, a band of land spirits followed it down from the mountains. *This was no good at all!* The wizard quickly gave a flip of his mighty tail and swam as fast as he could back to the ocean.

He only had one more placed left to check. Surely, there would be a safe place where he could explore the island. Now, more than

ever, he wanted to find a way to help the king invade this land! He had been chased away by a dragon, a giant eagle and now a huge bull.

Someone needed to get rid of these monsters and make this island safe! There must be a way, he thought, as he swam to the southern tip of the island. This was a place known for having whales, so the wizard thought his disguise would keep him safe here.

He swam past the small towns on the coast and saw the capital city, Reykjavik in the distance. He swam into the bay and stopped. He raised himself up as far as he could from the water to try and look at the shore.

Was it safe? He joined a group of whales and swam in circles with them, jumping and diving in the water. It seemed all quiet on shore. Maybe this was the perfect place for an army to launch an attack. The wizard swam closer to shore, leaving his whale friends in the ocean.

He moved closer to land, and as his feet touched the sand, he quickly changed back to his human wizard form. His shifty eyes darted back and forth.

He rubbed his hands gleefully as he whispered to himself "Yes, the King can launch his attack from here!" No sooner had the words left his lips, a powerful rumbling sounded and the ground under his feet shook and rocks tumbled.

The wizard looked up and a huge mountain giant appeared over the cliffs. His head was higher than the mountain tops, and as the wizard watched, the giant used an iron staff to step right over the tall mountains. The ground shook and there was a thunderous noise with each step. Just the sight of this terrible monster made the wizard long for his home in Denmark.

The wizard ran for the water, quickly changing back into his whale form. As he looked back, the mountain giant was now surrounded by many other beasts of all sizes and types. He swam quickly away, barely escaping as the giant's huge hand snapped down to grab him.

This would not do at all. This country of Iceland was protected on all sides. There was no way they could launch an attack! The wizard had no choice but to return to the King and tell him of all the mighty Guardians of Iceland that kept the people and magical inhabitants safe. To this day, no one has attacked or defeated the Guardians.

.

HULDUFÓLK - THE HIDDEN FOLK

It is common knowledge for those in the know that there are fairies in many forests. There are certainly leprechauns in Ireland. Elves are to be found at the North Pole, and most assuredly, there is a sea creature in the Lochs of Scotland. Perhaps somewhere out there you might also find a dragon, or even a unicorn. But the oldest and possibly the most magical creatures around are the Huldufolk of Iceland. Their story goes as far back as recorded time itself.

At the beginning of everything, there was a beautiful garden that stretched as far as the eye could see. In this garden, there lived a man named Adam and a woman named Eve. Adam and Eve had many children. During the day, the children explored and played while their parents enjoyed the garden and took long walks.

The children were all curious and loved to explore beyond the garden. Some of the best places were the rocky shoreline and caves and along the riverbeds. They spent hours playing and every day ventured further and further but always came back before the sun set. At the end of every day, Adam and Eve would gather the children to have dinner and they would all spend their evenings together. It was a very pleasant and happy life.

One day, Eve told the children they were having a special guest coming to dinner that night. She told them she wanted them to all be on their best behaviors. She instructed each of them to watch the sun in the sky and be home when it was starting to touch the treetops. That way, they would all have time for baths and be cleaned up to meet the special guest that evening.

Each of the children agreed and went their separate ways to play for the day. One group of the children followed one of the many streams, exploring the waters and looking at rocks and all sorts of shiny pebbles. They followed a path up a hill, scrambling over rocks and sliding through muddy parts as they went. At the top of the hill, they found some unusual lumps and bumps in the ground. They were curious to know what these were and where they came from. They looked closer.

Each of the mounds seemed to have tiny holes, like frozen bubbles that rock had grown solid around. Some of the mounds looked like piles of mud, sort of oozing, but solid. They were fascinated by these strange rocks and excited to explore the large field that stretched out before them. Some of the rocks were bare and ragged, some topped by a soft-looking green covering. The green covering was springy to the touch but seemed to be fragile. They carefully stepped around those parts as they continued to explore so as not to disturb the pretty green fluff.

They were having so much fun that they never noticed the sun was high in the sky. When the sun was starting to touch the treetops, their Mamma Eve had said that was when they were supposed to head home. However, they were so involved in their exploring, they did not watch the movement of the sun. They explored little caves and caverns, valleys and hilltops before they realized they were hungry.

"Oh my goodness, look at the sun," exclaimed one boy.

"It is so low in the sky," his sister said.

"We must hurry back," a third chimed in.

They rushed back home, retracing their steps as quickly as they could. They slipped and slid in the mud, caught sticks and leaves in their hair, and snagged and tore their clothing as they ran pell-mell towards their home in the garden.

As they reached the garden where their mother waited, they were breathless and dirty. Eve was relieved to see them return home safe, but was very upset with them. The sun was nearly setting and their special guest would be arriving soon. There was no time to take a bath and change into clean clothes.

Eve would be so embarrassed for anyone to see the children so muddy and their clothes torn. Most of the time, she was proud of her beautiful children. Tonight, she had so many lined up all clean with their bright shiny face, it made this group look even worse. It might be best to just hide them. She thought there were so many children that no one would notice if a few were missing, especially if they had never met them. Hiding them would be better than showing them so dirty and bedraggled.

She thought quickly and said to the small group, "Go, children – go back out of the garden and play in the field until it is dark and then come home." She went quickly to their food stock and took out handfuls of bread and cheese. Giving some to each of the children, she hugged them and sent them on their way.

The small group obeyed their mother and followed the stream back to the rocky field. Eve gathered the remaining children and went to meet Adam and have their dinner.

The special guest arrived and asked Eve, "Where are the rest of your children?"

Eve replied, "These are all the children."

Adam nodded in agreement and led their guest away to look at the beautiful trees and flowers in the garden. The evening passed as they walked together and then sat to have dinner. After a pleasant meal, their guest thanked them for the food and the visit with their family. As he was leaving, Eve thought she heard him whisper the strangest thing.

"Whatever has been hidden from me, shall be hidden from all people."

Eve thought she must have heard wrong, shook her head and thought no more about the odd comment. She walked to the edge of the garden and called to her small group of missing children. Dusk had fallen and it would be fully dark soon. She frowned as she looked, but did not see them. Just then, she heard their voices and turned quickly, thinking they were behind her.

"Hello?" she called, "where are you?"

To her surprise, she could hear giggling and laughing but could not see a single child.

She jumped as she heard several voices cry "we're here, mom, we're here!" but as she looked around, she saw no one.

"Where?" she asked, "I can hear you but I can't see you," she said, looking from left to right as she searched for the children.

Her eyes grew wide as right in front of her, the group of children appeared. Slowly, shimmering, at first almost transparent, then their forms becoming solid and clear. She stared at them, for while they had always been pretty children, now, somehow, they were even more beautiful. Their hair shone like gold and each one's was perfectly arranged. Their faces were all clean and bright and their skin had an angelic glow. The clothing they now wore was like nothing she had ever seen before, it was very finely made and of the most beautiful cloth. Each had on a tunic and pants that were brightly colored, the edges lined in silver and gold. She reached out to touch the arm of the child nearest to her and the fabric had the softest texture she had ever felt.

These were her children, and familiar to her, but somehow strange at the same time. She looked at them, confused.

"You look like my children, but not quite," she said slowly, "tell me now, are you changelings?"

She looked around the small circle, searching the faces of the children. They all seemed to smile sadly. One stepped forward, and reached to hug her.

"Mother, dear, we all love you very much," the beautiful girl said, "we are all still your children, but we have changed now."

"Yes," said a boy, every bit as handsome as the girl was beautiful, "when we left the garden, we went out and were playing in the field. We cannot explain it, but we all felt a strange sensation. It was like a tingle and a shiver and we knew something was different."

"Yes," their mother said, nodding.

"We can hear each other's thoughts, and as you approached here, we could hear your thoughts as well," the girl explained. "The visitor tonight told you we were hidden from people, what does that mean mother? We are not Hidden – look, we're right here!"

"I didn't understand it before," Eve said slowly, "but I think I'm beginning to realize what has happened." She looked at the small circle of children and continued, "you are Hidden most of the time and can only be seen by ordinary humans when you want to be, when you concentrate. The rest of the time, I think you will be invisible to everyone except each other."

They all looked at each other, and then one by one, the children each began to smile. Their new ability to speak to each other in their minds made it possible to communicate quickly. The idea of being invisible whenever they wanted sounded quite fun.

Eve smiled and hugged each of them and said, "My beautiful children, you are special now and I will always love you, even when I can't see you. Let's get you all home."

Together, they went back to their home in the garden. Eve and the small group of children shared their discovery with Adam and the rest of the family. Adam hugged each of them, assuring them he also still loved them very much. Their other brothers and sisters, though, seemed uncertain and a little afraid to get too close.

Over the next few weeks, the group of children that Eve had come to think of as Huldufolk, or Hidden People, spent more and more time exploring the world beyond the garden and became quite at home in the rocky field with the moss-covered stones. Each day when they came home, they tried to share stories of their adventures with their other brothers and sisters.

Each time, their siblings seemed unwilling to listen. They did not want to spend time anymore with the ones their mother called Huldufolk. Day after day, they tried, but the groups didn't seem to have much in common anymore.

As the years passed, the Huldufolk spent less and less time with their other brothers and sisters, and less time in the garden that had been their home. They eventually made their home among the rocks of the field and the cliffs by the sea. They became protective of the land and did not allow humans to harm it. They did not like rocks to be moved, or the moss to be disturbed, nor did they like anyone to come too close to their homes.

Sometimes, they would go visit the humans to see if they would be welcomed. The Huldufolk became generous with gifts and rewards for hospitality, but misfortune often fell on those who were selfish or inhospitable.

The Hidden's ability to remain invisible made it easy for them to confuse humans and bring misfortune or bad luck. If a human angered or offended one of the Hidden, the human often misplaced tools, lost supplies or even had holes mysteriously appear in their shoes or all their fish become rotten.

To this day, any time an Icelander meets a stranger, they make sure to always be polite and courteous, sharing food and lodging freely, especially if the stranger is unusually beautiful. You can never be sure if it's one of the Huldufolk.

THE CHANGELING

This story started in Vopnafjörður, (wop-na-fyore-thur) according to a very old woman who knew everything about this sort of thing.

In a magical, mist-shrouded kingdom, the first monarch of the Hidden lived in the Thule. The Thule was not visible from outside the kingdom, so it was protected. In these early days, life was peaceful and happy. The king and queen of the land were well-liked by all their subjects. When they announced they were having a child, everyone was very happy.

When the child was born, she was the most beautiful baby anyone had ever seen, or even imagined. Her rainbow-hued hair curled in tight ringlets, encircling her head like a coronet. Her skin sparkled and shimmered. Each freckle she had was made up of the lightest hues of pink, purple, blue and green.

She was the most extraordinary and unique baby anyone had ever seen. The King and Queen decided that they must choose an exceptional name for their exceptional child. They took their time in choosing just the right one.

When the beautiful baby was four days old, she still had no name. The King and Queen sat in their throne room considering all the possible names.

"Arnbjorg… or maybe Brimhildur?" The King suggested.

"How about Elingunnur, or the name Kristborg is quite pretty," The Queen said thoughtfully.

"Villimey perhaps? The name we choose must be as beautiful and unique as our daughter is, for certain," he replied.

They were interrupted by a member of the guard, announcing

the arrival of Elf Queen Borghildur of Alaborg. This was quite an honor. The Elf Queen was very powerful and did not often leave her home in the forest. As the Elf Queen entered, the King was surprised at her serious look. She walked up to his throne and leaned close, capturing his full attention.

"I have come to warn you of an attack the trolls are planning," she said quietly.

"What?" the King said, shocked, "why would trolls attack my kingdom?"

"I have knowledge of a scheme surrounding your daughter. If they replace the young princess with a troll changeling, one day when she becomes Queen, they will be able to take over and rule the kingdom."

The King was happy the Elf Queen learned of the plot and came to warn him. He knew the Elf Queen would not have come herself, unless she could provide him with the way to defeat the trolls.

"How would they accomplish such a thing?"

"Troll magic for a changeling is usually easy, but this case is special and more difficult. For their plan to work, the changeling must be able to take your daughter's place and convince everyone in the kingdom. Since she is so beautiful and so very unique, it will take more time. They need to keep her and the changeling together while the trolls chant her name until the changeling looks exactly like her. Then, the changeling would take over the baby's place and no one would be able to tell the difference."

"How do we stop them?" the Queen asked, very concerned about her new daughter. She had been listening carefully to the conversation between the Elf Queen and the King.

"Her true name must be kept a secret so that the troll cannot chant it. You must call her by a different name to protect her."

"Name her secretly, but call her something else?" the queen asked.

"The child's name must not be spoken aloud and should not be recorded. Her guardian angel must be the only one to know her true name, while she is called by a different name."

The King and Queen agreed. The Elf Queen consulted the little girl's guardian angel and the angel chose a very special name.

To the kingdom, the princess was known as Snotra. This was her elf name. It was a name with a magical charm that would protect her all through her life.

Her true name will remain a secret until the end of days. And this was how the Elf Queen thwarted the trolls' plan.

NOW I SHOULD LAUGH

In the early days of Iceland, there were three sisters named Árna, Lísabet, and Tala, who lived in a valley near Lake Mývatn (me' vot). They were all married and when their parents died, the sisters were each left with an equal portion of the estate. Among the valuables the parents left to them was a gold ring. Each of them wanted the ring, but they could not come up with a fair way to decide who should have it.

Finally, they agreed on a contest. Since their father had been a well-known prankster who loved playing tricks, they decided a challenge in his memory would determine which of them would get the ring. The one among them who could play the biggest joke on her husband would be the winner.

They sat down and drew up four simple rules. One, they would have a month to plan, playing their pranks on Easter Sunday; two, they would each have to get their husbands in front of everyone during church; three, the biggest reaction from the townsfolk would decide the winner; and four, they would tell no one of their contest. They all decided this was fair and agreed to the plan.

During Lent, Árna began to prepare for Easter by sitting down to spin wool into fabric for a new suit. Her husband came in from the field and asked what she was doing.

"Gunnar, dear, can't you see?" she asked, confused.

"No," he said. "I see you move your hands as if you were working, but I don't see anything."

"What I'm spinning," Árna said, "is from the highest quality fiber I have ever seen, it is so fine it is transparent right now. But, when I am finished, you will have the finest suit ever made to wear at Easter."

Gunnar trusted her and felt silly questioning her. Every day, he saw her hands moving as if she were working, but he never saw any yarn or thread.

At the same time, the second sister, Lísabet, became depressed and sad. Her husband Baldur asked her what ailed her.

"It makes me sad to see you so sick," she said.

"Sick? Me?" Baldur replied, "No, I feel fine."

"How can you say that?" replied Lísabet, "You're so pale and you have circles under your eyes. Anyone can see you're very sick."

He looked at her strangely, shook his head, and returned to the field to work, thinking she was being silly.

The third sister, Tala, was married to a man named Dómar, whose voice was so dreadful and grating that no one could stand his singing. He was completely tone-deaf and could not carry a tune at all.

Over breakfast, Tala asked her husband Dómar to join her in singing a special for Easter Sunday service. "It would mean so much to me, my dear."

Dómar stared at her. "What? You know I never sing! I *can't* sing. Why, when I was a boy and wanted to sing with the choir, they kicked me out because my singing was so loud and off-key I made the entire group sound bad. I went out alone to the fields and when I started to practice, the birds took off in flight, the sheep scattered and my poor dog ran off. I found him later, hiding under the bed moaning."

"Don't be silly, I love your singing. We have weeks to practice together and in fact, we shall start today," she said firmly.

He looked at her as if she was crazy, but just nodded. And so, their singing practice began.

One day, Árna announced the spinning was complete and that she had begun to weave the fabric. Gunnar still did not see anything that she was working on.

The same day, Lísabet commented again on how sick Baldur looked. He insisted he felt fine, but she continued to fret and finally broke down in tears. They did not have a mirror for him to see his reflection, but he told her again he felt fine.

"Please, please, go back to bed and rest," she pleaded, "I just can't bear to see you so weak and sallow."

She was so convincing, Baldur began to believe he might truly be ill, so he agreed to go back to bed.

For days, she told him each morning on how terrible he looked. She would only allow him to have broth to eat and insisted he stay in bed. Lísabet insisted that he was getting weaker and weaker, while he protested that his health was fine.

Tala and Dómar went out far past the edge of the village each day to practice singing. Each day, Tala would stuff her ears with cotton to drown out Dómar's hideous voice.

This went on until shortly before Easter.

Árna excitedly declared the fabric was done and that she had started sewing his new suit. Gunnar never saw a scrap of fabric. A few days before Easter, Árna said the suit was ready.

Across town, Lísabet was absolutely grief-stricken. Baldur tried to comfort her, asking why she was so upset.

"You've been so sick, and, oh, now you're dead."

"I am not!" he insisted. "I'm as much alive as you or anybody else."

"Oh no, you're dead all right," she sobbed, crying her eyes out.

She carried on until she convinced him that he really was dead and he must be a ghost. She had him lay on the table, and called for the carpenter to make a coffin for him. Lísabet made the arrangements for Baldur's funeral service to be on Easter Sunday.

When Easter Sunday arrived, Árna came up to Gunnar and began to fuss about him, telling him that she was dressing him in his beautiful new suit. Gunnar said he felt naked, but she replied it was just because the suit was so exquisite.

Lísabet had Baldur coffined, but left him a small hole at the head so he could see. That done, he was carted off to the church, lying in the coffin.

Tala and Dómar were preparing to leave for church as well and Tala was humming.

"I'm really not sure about this," Dómar said.

Tala smiled and patted his arm, "It's not that bad. I will be with you and I'm sure no one will run off and hide under a bed moaning like your dog."

He replied, "Oh, no! Truly, if not moaning, then everyone will start laughing!"

"Nonsense, you sing beautifully," she answered.

Baldur was lying in his coffin at the front of the church. Tala took Dómar by the hand and they walked to the front by Lísabet. As Dómar started to sing, there were murmurs and quiet laughter.

As they walked into the church, Árna said to Gunnar, "Let us go up and sing with Dómar to drown out that horrible voice." She then pulled him to the front of the church.

So, Gunnar walked to the front and started to sing. Dómar was singing so forcefully that his arms were pumping and his hands flying about. He took one look at Gunnar with his transparent clothing and the songbook went flying out of his hands. The murmur in the church grew louder and everyone began looking at each other. They all started laughing. It was difficult to tell if they were laughing at Gunnar or Dómar.

Lifting his head, Baldur, lying in his coffin, saw Gunnar naked and at the same time heard the horrible wailing of Dómar. He could no longer contain himself and exclaimed, "Now I should laugh! Truly, I would be laughing so hard at you two right now if I weren't dead!"

Hearing his words, Gunnar and Dómar realized the prank. Dómar stopped singing in mid-phrase, while Gunnar scrambled to the door, knowing he wasn't wearing a stitch of clothing. The church service went on as if nothing happened.

Baldur continued to lie there in the coffin until the sermon was over, and then he climbed out. Everyone laughed at how all three of them had been tricked, but agreed Baldur was the most gullible. His wife was voted the winner and was presented with the ring.

And that's the end of this story.

.

THE FIELD HAND

A young man named Dreki was from the southern peninsula of Iceland. One summer, he traveled to the North to find work as a field hand. His travel was uneventful until he reached the heathlands. A heathlands is an area of rocky ground, where little can grow except a heath moss. It is dry and the ground is covered in hummocks, which are lumps and mounds that are often home to the Hidden Folk. As Dreki rode into the heathlands, a heavy fog rolled in that was so thick he soon lost his way.

The dense fog was followed by a cold sleet, so Dreki decided to stop for the night and pitch his tent. After his camp was set up, he dug into his pack, pulled out his food and began to eat.

While he was enjoying his meal, he heard a pitiful whining outside the tent. Getting up to look, he found a shivering hound, soaking wet and looking hungry. He was surprised to see a dog there because he hadn't seen a farm or house in quite a while. The animal was so ugly and odd-looking that Dreki was a little afraid to have it in his tent. But, he felt sorry for the poor thing, so he patted the ground, inviting the dog inside. He gave the dog all it wanted to eat. The mutt wolfed down the food and then left, disappearing into the fog. Dreki finished his dinner and lay down, using his saddle as a pillow. After his long day, he quickly fell asleep.

He dreamed that a very beautiful woman entered the tent. She wore fine clothing and was surrounded by a shimmering glow. She moved silently and in his dream he looked into her eyes. They sparkled brightly as she smiled at him. He knew then that he was meeting one of the Hidden Folk. Her eyes were full of wisdom and she seemed quite old, although there wasn't a line or wrinkle on her face that showed her age.

"You were kind to the animal that came to your tent tonight. That was my daughter. I want to thank you for your kindness and generosity," she said. "I am sorry I cannot reward you the way I think you deserve. But I'd like you to accept this scythe, which has been my own. It will always remain sharp whether it cuts hay or grass. It will allow you to cut faster by yourself than an entire group of men working together. But beware and follow these rules: Never reveal its magic to anyone, never lend because it will work only for you, and never tell the story of how you came to have it. It has strong magic, and I believe it will be of some use to you."

Then the woman disappeared and Dreki slept peacefully for the rest of the night.

When he awoke the next day, he saw the fog was gone. It was bright daylight and the sun was high in the sky. He moved around his camp, packing up to continue his journey. Dreki fetched his horses and folded his tent, packing it away. He began to load his supplies and harness the horses. When he picked up his saddle, he found a scythe lying under it, looking a bit worn and rusty but still in good shape.

He remembered his dream about the Hidden woman, and realized it wasn't a dream after all. He carefully wrapped the scythe and packed it away. He saddled his horse and headed down the road. The rest of his journey was uneventful and he quickly reached the nearest settlement where he started looking for work. It was almost a full week into the haymaking season. All the farmers had already hired the help they needed. He began to get discouraged.

At the last farm, one of the field hands suggested he might try the widow woman's farm on the far side of town. She hadn't hired on any field hands yet, so he may have luck getting a job there.

"She hasn't hired anyone at all?" Dreki asked. "Doesn't she need help?"

"Oh, she does!" the man replied, shaking his head up and down vigorously, "Every year, she doesn't hire anyone until at least a week or two after everyone else. The strange thing is, her fields are always finished the same time the rest of us are, and always has a good amount of hay. She is shrewd, and quite rich, and most years will hire someone for only a week, but never pays any wages."

"How does all the work get done with so little help?" Dreki was confused.

"I don't know, but I guess there's no harm in talking with her since no one else is hiring."

The helpful farm hand waved and turned back to his work.

Deciding he had no choice, Dreki set off to find the widow woman and inquire about a job.

He arrived at the house, and quickly found the widow woman. She agreed to allow him to work for a week, but insisted on one rule.

"You will work all week, mowing the hay, and I will rake it all on Saturday. You must mow more during the week than I can rake on Saturday. If you don't, I won't pay you anything."

Dreki thought this was a fair deal. He knew he was strong and he was a hard worker. There would be no way this woman could rake more in one day than he could mow in five! He quickly agreed and started working that same day. The widow woman agreed to provide a cot in the barn to sleep in, and three meals a day, so Dreki was pleased with the deal.

Getting right to work, he used the scythe that the Hidden woman had given him. He found it cut quite well and he was able to work quickly. He cut hay for five days straight and did not have to stop and sharpen the blade.

On Friday afternoon, he went into a building called the smithy, which was the blacksmith's shop where tools were made and stored. He was surprised to see a huge stock of rakes and a large pile of snaths. Dreki wondered why there was a pile of the handles without the scythe attached. He thought this farm certainly had a lot of tools for having no workers. Shrugging to himself, he picked out what he needed and returned to the field.

That night he dreamt of the Hidden woman who had given him the scythe. In his dream, she said to him, "You have worked hard all week and have cut a great deal of grass. But it won't take the widow long to rake it all up. If she rakes all you have cut by the end of tomorrow, she will fire you and not pay you any wages."

Dreki nodded and the Hidden continued, "Watch how she's working and if you think she will catch up to you, go to the smithy for more tools. Take as many of the snaths as you can carry, tie scythes to them, then take them out to the field with you. See how it goes."

Dreki woke up, and he was all alone. He wondered about the strange words of the Hidden woman. *"See how it goes? What could she have meant by that?"* he thought as he headed out to the field to begin mowing. Around midmorning, the widow came to the field, carrying five rakes.

"You have cut quite a bit," his employer said, "more than I thought you would."

Then she laid the rakes here and there around the field, keeping one rake in her hand. She began raking. Dreki watched with his eyes wide as all four rakes stood upright and raked along with the one in the widow's hands. As much as she raked, the other rakes did even more.

Dreki stopped quickly for lunch and rushed back to work. By mid-afternoon he realized the widow and her five rakes were too fast. By the end of the day, she would be able to rake all the hay it had taken him five days to cut.

Remembering what the Hidden woman had told him in his dream, he headed to the smithy and grabbed several snaths. He tied scythes to them, took them to the field where he was cutting and scattered them in the grass. When he picked up his scythe that the Hidden woman had given him and started to swing, the rest jumped to life and started swinging in the same motion. He and his extra scythes cut through the hay quickly. By evening, Dreki was tired but had more hay cut than his employer could rake. She came to him in the field, carrying her rakes with her.

"Come along, Dreki," she said, "bring the scythes and we'll put all these tools away. You've done well this week. I can see you know more of things than I had expected."

"Thank you ," he replied, thinking he had the Hidden to thank for his knowledge.

"I am pleased," the widow said, "As a reward, you may work here for me as long as you like."

Dreki stayed for the rest of the summer. He worked alongside the widow woman and although they took their time, they made a lot of hay that year. When the fall came, she paid him a great sum of money. The next summer and for many summers after that, Dreki came back to work in the widow woman's field.

GISSUR OF BOTNAR

In the Norwest peninsula, there are two mountains named Bjolfell (be-yoll-fell) and Burfell, which are separated by a river. In the early days of Iceland, there were two trolls that lived in these mountains. They were sisters and lived across the river from each other, one on each of the mountaintops. The sisters were very close and both often crossed the river to visit the other. The trollwife of Burfell put two large, flat, free-standing rocks in the river as stepping stones so she and her sister wouldn't have to get their feet wet when crossing. For them, it took three hops to get across the river. The rocks came to be known as Trollwife's Leap.

Nearby, there is a well-worn trail, used by many people who traveled north to the mountain pastures. It was common to use this trail going to round up sheep, fish in the mountain lakes, hunt for swans, or dig up roots for medicine.

One summer, a famer named Gissur went up to the mountain to fish in one of the lakes. He rode his horse and led a pack horse loaded with supplies. He camped for several days at the lake and caught a great many fish. After he broke camp, he loaded the pack horse with the fish he had caught and set off for home.

The trip was uneventful until he neared the mountain pass near Trollwife's Leap. Suddenly, he heard a booming voice echo out from the top of Mount Burfell.

"Lend me a pot, sister!" he heard the shrieking voice cry.

"What do you want with it?" answered a horrible voice from across the river.

Gissur knew he was listening to the trollwives and was quite afraid. They were quite well known and he had hoped to pass through the mountain without running into either of them. His fear grew stronger when he heard the first trollwife reply.

"I would like to cook man-stew in it."

"You have caught a man in these parts?" yelled the second trollwife.

The first answered, "I see the man Gissur of Botnar in the canyon and will catch him for the stew."

Gissur was terrified now. He saw a huge ugly trollwife scrambling down Mount Burfell and heading straight for him. She looked very hungry and he knew she would make him into man-stew for certain if she caught him. He let go of the pack horse so that he could run, and he let his own horse run at full speed. He never looked back or touched the reins. He just let the animal run as fast and it could go, knowing this horse was faster than any other he had ever owned.

As fast as his horse ran, Gissur could feel the hot stinky breath of the trollwife on the back of his neck as she was gaining on them. He took the most direct route he could, straight down the mountain, with the trollwife on his heels the entire way.

As he neared the town of Klofi, he saw that the townspeople had gathered and were watching as he and the trollwife raced toward them. The villagers knew there was no time to lose and rushed to ring all the church bells just as Gissur reached the homefield fence.

The trollwife realized her dinner was lost, and she screamed as she threw her ax at him, but just then, the bells of the church clamored and pealed. She screamed, her hands grasping her head in pain, and the ax fell harmlessly short of Gissur and his horse.

The sound of the bells caused the trollwife to go mad and she ran off, back up the mountain as fast as she could. She jumped over farmers in their fields and tripped over sheep as they grazed while she lumbered and limped back in the direction of the canyon by Mount Burfell.

A few days later, she was found dead, turned into solid rock by the sun. On that day, the canyon was renamed for her, and has been known ever since as Trollwife's Canyon.

GRÝLA AND
JÓLAKÖTTURINN, THE CHRISTMAS CAT

In the far mountains of Iceland, way up in the north, there is a place that no one dares go. There are no roads, just paths worn from the feet of sheep and a few other creatures. There are steep cliffs and rocky parts, all filled with caves and hidden places. This is home to one particular troublesome and terrible troll. Her name is Gryla (gree-la) and she is a hideous creature, half-ogre and half-troll. She and her troll-husband Leppalúði (Lep-a-luthi) live in the Dimmuborgir lava fields with their many children.

Like most trolls, she was mean and bad-tempered. She slobbered and snorted, she smelled bad and was generally unpleasant in every way imaginable. But, she was also known in the troll world to be a wonderful cook. Other trolls made any excuse to visit and stay for dinner, often requesting a particular dish, her specialty. She was most famous for her Bad Kids Stew.

She spent most of her time searching for and collecting the main ingredient for her famous stew – bad children. She looked for the laziest ones who didn't do chores, gave their parents trouble or the children that played mean pranks. Gryla had a special skill in finding these children. She has thirteen ears on each side of her head, which gave her excellent hearing, even across very far distances. She could hear the moaning and groaning, and the complaints of lazy children who didn't want to do their chores. Sometimes she would go herself, and sometimes she would send one of her troll-children to snatch the human child up. They would be careful not to be seen, stuffing the child into a sack to carry back to the mountains where Gryla would keep them in a cave prison until she made her Bad Kids Stew.

Gryla often could not get to all the bad children because the days in Iceland are so short in the summertime. Any troll caught out in sunlight would turn to rock, so they could only move about the country for the few hours of darkness each night. For all those lazy children they couldn't get to, Gryla would carefully write their names down so she could find and steal them in the fall and winter. They had the most time to collect the bad children during the long nights of December. Soon, thirteen of Gryla's troll-boys became known as the Yule Lads because they came to the villages around Christmas.

But, many times Gryla went alone to collect the bad children for her stew pot. She was often seen in the moonlight dragging a sack, closely followed by a monstrous-looking cat. The stories of Gryla's horrible ugliness were legendary. Everyone seemed to see her just a little differently. Some said she had hooves where her feet should have been and ran hunched over. Others said she had fifteen tails that stuck out in every direction from under her skirts. Still others described a face covered with warts and a crooked smile showing three rotting teeth. But all the stories had one thing in common – she always wore an odd hood that covered her head and hung down around her shoulders, stopping just at the top of her arm. It was much too big to be a scarf and far too short to be a proper cloak.

One cold winter's night, Gryla was out to fill her bag with a few mean children. She was planning to have company for dinner the next week and wanted to serve her Bad Kids Stew.

Her pet walked by her side. The ugly little animal had his own special way of sniffing out the laziest children. He would lurk around after the sheep roundup each fall, waiting for the shearing.

Gryla always sent him to steal wool so she wouldn't have to shear her own sheep. Gryla wove many clothes with magic protection spells and needed a lot of wool. The cat would watch for unguarded bags and steal as many as he could. He noticed that everyone that helped with the shearing, or worked the wool into yarn or cloth was rewarded with new clothes just before Christmas. So, Gryla's cat liked to find those children who didn't get new clothes at Christmas because those were the laziest. All he had to do around

Christmas was look for those who wore old clothes. Because of this, he soon became known as Jólakötturinn (yola-cut-ter-rin), The Christmas Cat.

On this winter's night, Gryla and the Christmas Cat had visited the homes of two lazy children, stealing them from their beds and tossing them in bags Gryla carried over her shoulder. She was tired and decided to only collect one more tonight and that would make a good stew for her company dinner. They tromped along, soon arriving at the small house at the foot of the mountain. Jólakötturinn ran up the side of the turf roof and down into the wooden smoke hole. Jumping down onto the table inside, he used his nose to push open the window for Gryla to reach inside.

The cat jumped outside as Gryla reached toward the sleeping child, snatching her up in one long bony hand. The little girl's eyes flew open and she instantly knew it was the horrible ogre Gryla that had come to steal her away.

Before she could shout a warning and wake the household, Gryla had pulled her through the window and run off down the road, the little girl tucked under her arm. Her long troll legs took huge steps and in no time they were several miles away from the farmhouse. Gryla stopped to shove her prize into a bag, but the little girl fought, kicking and punching. Gryla was very surprised because most children were so frightened they were no trouble at all. This one was different. She wriggled and wrestled, her little hands flying in Gryla's face. The girl's hand grabbed at Gryla's hood and snatched it off her head.

Shocked, Gryla dropped the other two sacks she had been carrying. Two boys promptly jumped out, joining the fight. Gryla fell to the ground and all three children ran as fast as they could, the little girl still tightly holding on to the hood. Gryla watched them run and she sneered, annoyed. The hood had been woven with a very special spell, one that changed her appearance.

When she wore it, everyone saw a horrible monster, which was hardly at all how she normally looked. Without her magic hood, people would see her as an ordinary troll and would not be afraid of her. She might be captured or caught in the sunlight, which would turn her to stone. Children would no longer be afraid and instead would shout at her presence or fight back if she tried to steal them.

Frustrated at the loss of her Bad Kids Stew ingredients, and even more upset at the loss of her hood, Gryla had no choice but to return home to the mountain cave. A short time later, her magic spindle was stolen and she was never able to make a new magic hood. She spent the rest of her days in the mountains, away from anyone who could see her, and never again made Bad Kids Stew.

OF MARBENDILL

On the southwestern peninsula of Iceland, just south of the capital city of Reykjavik, there is a small farming village called Vogar, which means "Creeks". It has always been one of the best places in southern Iceland for small-boat fishing.

There was a farmer named Kolur who lived in Vogar and was an avid fisherman. One day, he had been out for several hours and had little success, when he felt something heavy on his hook. Carefully, he hauled in the line, and as he pulled it into the boat, he saw a large shape coming out of the water.

He thought he had caught a mighty sea creature. He heaved and struggled and finally pulled it aboard. Kolur was surprised to find that it seemed to be an odd man with a long flat tail who stared up at him from the floor of his boat.

"Who are you? What kind of man are you that you would be floating in the sea and get caught on my fishing line?" Kolur stuttered, confused.

"I am not a man," his catch said angrily, "I am a Marbendill, from the seafloor."

"Marbendill?" Kolur said, "A merman?"

"Yes, I was fixing the chimney on my mother's home when your hook snagged me." The Marbendill said, "Now please let me down again so I can finish."

Kolur pondered this for a moment. "No," he said, "I don't think I'll let you go just yet. You'll stay with me."

Kolur had never seen a Marbendill before but he had heard stories. A Marbendill would avoid human contact and conversation as much as possible. It was said that the Merman could see things a

31

mortal could not and often had knowledge of the future. He had heard that it was difficult to get one to talk, but if he could, the advice would be worth a great deal.

It was no surprise to Kolur when the Marbendill refused to speak any more to him. When the morning turned into noon, Kolur finished his fishing. He rowed ashore, taking the Marbendill with him. After he had pulled up his boat, his dog came running to greet him and jumped up at him excitedly. Annoyed, Kolur pushed the dog away.

The Marbendill laughed. Kolur looked at him strangely, but said nothing.

As they headed up through his hayfield to his house, Kolur stumbled over a hummock and cursed it. The Marbendill laughed again. Kolur looked at him again, but still said nothing.

When Kolur reached his house, he sat down to the noon meal with his overseer. They discussed the running of the farm, the yield of the hayfield, and herd of sheep. He had faith in the man who had been with him for years. The overseer said the hayfield crop was poor and they had lost a number of sheep. Kolur was discouraged by this bad news.

"Well, we have no choice but to continue on. I'm sure under your good management things will improve," Kolur said.

The Marbendill laughed once again.

Turning to the merman, Kolur said, "You have laughed at me three times now, tell me why."

"No," said Marbendill, "Not until you promise to take me back to the spot in the ocean where you pulled me in."

Kolur promised that he would and went outside with the Marbendill to hear what he had to say.

The Marbendill was not happy, but he gave Kolur his answer. "I laughed because you do not understand or value the best things in life, and you fail to see the positive. But, you accept without question those things that should make you wonder."

"I laughed the first time," said Marbendill, "when you kicked your dog, the one creature in the world who is always happy to see you. I laughed the second time when you tripped over the hummock and swore, because the hummock covers buried treasure. The third time I laughed was when you responded with such understanding to your overseer's excuses. He has been lying and he steals from you."

The merman folded his arms and demanded, "Now, keep your promise and take me back where you pulled me from."

"Well now," replied Kolur, "I have no way of knowing for certain if my dog is always happy to see me, and I don't know how to check the loyalty of my overseer. But, I can go see if there is gold or treasure under the hummock. If there is, then I will take you back to the ocean. If you are right about the treasure, I will believe the other things are true too."

Kolur took a shovel and dug up the hummock, while the Marbendill stood nearby watching. In a short time, the shovel hit something solid. He dug it up and found a large chest filled with gold. The Marbendill had told him the truth. Kolur was so happy he immediately took the merman back on his boat to the spot where he had pulled him in.

Before he jumped back into the water, the Marbendill said, "You have done a good thing returning me to my home. In time, I will reward you. You must learn the lesson from our time today, and recognize the opportunity. Farewell, my friend."

Kolur watched the Marbendill dive into the ocean, and that was the last he ever saw of the merman.

A few weeks later, Kolur was quite happy. His dog went everywhere with him, he had replaced the overseer and was enjoying life as a wealthy man. As he and the dog were taking a morning walk along the shoreline one day, he saw a seabull and several seagray cows on the shore adjoining his land. A seagray cow on land was very rare. It was a special type of cow that had a balloon-like sack around its nose so that it could breathe underwater.

Kolur knew instantly that this was a gift from the merman. If he could catch them and remove the balloons, they would be an excellent addition to his herd. He rushed to the seagray herd, thinking if he captured the bull, the cows would follow. But it was too fast for him and Kolur only caught the closest cow. As he removed the sack so she could not return to the sea, the rest of the herd stampeded for the water. All but that one cow jumped back into the ocean.

Kolur was very pleased with the Marbendill's gift because that cow turned out to be one of the best that ever grazed in Iceland. A great breed of cattle descended from her and spread over most of the country. As for Kolur, he lived a long and happy life with his dog.

THE HIRED HAND AND THE LAKE DWELLERS

There once was a rich farmer who had a large flock of sheep. They fed on green grass in a beautiful field and drank from a pretty lake on the property. His hay fields grew plentiful crops. He had a snug barn that was home to his cows, horses and chickens. His farm was successful but he had a major problem.

Each year at Christmas, everyone would leave to visit family for the holidays, except one person. The shepherd always stayed alone for the holiday to look after the farm, the flock, and rest of the livestock. When everyone returned on Boxing Day, the day after Christmas, the shepherd would be missing. This happened every year. They searched high and low, but there was never any trace to be found. So, every year, right after Christmas, the farmer would hire a new shepherd.

This was quite a mystery. What happened at the farm every year? Why did the shepherds always disappear and where did they go? The farmer hoped each of the missing men had not suffered a grim fate. He had never seen a sign of a troll and didn't think the Hidden Folk were angry, but he worried about the missing men. Although he was concerned, the farmer had a large flock of sheep and needed a shepherd to tend to them, so every year he hired a new shepherd.

One year, a man named Kalli came to apply for the job. The farmer told Kalli the job was dangerous and that every other shepherd had disappeared. Kalli was not worried, but he saw the farmer was concerned. He promised he would be careful, so the farmer hired him.

Months passed, and Kalli did a good job as shepherd. He

enjoyed working for the farmer and his family. The farmer became fond of Kalli and was pleased with his work. Throughout the spring, summer, and fall, there was no trouble with trolls, Hidden Folk, or any other beings.

Soon it was winter and Christmas was only a few weeks away. The farmer began to worry about Kalli, thinking about all the other shepherds that had disappeared. As they planned for the holiday, the farmer told Kalli they would be gone for several days. He was worried and thought to cancel this year's travel.

Kalli scoffed and assured the farmer he would be fine. The farmer then begged Kalli to go with them, but Kalli would not leave the farm unguarded or the animals unattended for that long. The farmer did not want to take the risk of Kalli disappearing. Kalli would not change his mind. Before the farmer and his family left to travel across the mountain, he insisted Kalli stay in the main house for safety.

The farmer's house was spacious and beautiful. The large main room, the baðstofa (bath-stofa), had a wood floor and wood panels over the sod walls. Once everyone was gone, Kalli walked around the room to think. He began to plan. He had realized that while they didn't seem to have a troll problem, something was going on. It would be wise to plan for whatever might happen. The first thing he did was to light candles all around the baðstofa so it was very bright inside. Then, he started looking for a place to hide, just in case.

He looked around the room – all the furniture had legs and under any of it would not be a good hiding place. There was a cabinet in one corner and a cooking stove, but neither were far enough away from a wall for him to fit behind.

Finally, he pulled out two of the wood panels from one end of the room and squeezed himself in through the opening. When he put the panels back in place, he was completely hidden. He stood between the turf wall and the paneling, watching the baðstofa through a crack in the boards. From there, he could see his sheepdog laying asleep under one of the beds.

Many hours passed without incident. Kalli fell asleep and awoke to the sound of scratching. Squinting through the crack, he saw two big, gruesome-looking creatures moving around the room. They were eight feet tall, both hunched over because the ceiling was low for them. They had long stringy hair, sunken eyes, huge jaws and runny noses. They shuffled around the room, looking over everything, when one of them stopped and sniffed.

"Smells of humans. Ugh, it smells of humans," the creature said.

"Yow, but none here now," answered the other, swaying his head from side to side, his eyes rolling over every corner of the room.

He spotted the dog under the bed. Leaping that direction, he ducked down and slid on his knees the last couple of feet, until his massive head stuck right up under the bed.

The dog growled, but the creature growled back, even more fiercely than the dog. The poor hound yelped and took off like a shot out the open door. Kalli was so relieved he had found a good hiding place. He wasn't at all sure he wanted to face these two.

Satisfied they had the house to themselves, one of the creatures let out an ear-splitting whistle. Suddenly, the baðstofa filled with more of the creatures.

As Kalli watched from his hiding place, tables seemed to appear out of nowhere. They were covered with tablecloths, then heaped shiny silver plates and silverware. At one end of the table, one of the creatures had placed golden goblets encrusted with precious jewels. The tables were loaded with food and the creatures set down to a fantastic dinner.

Kalli could smell the meats and sausages. He saw bowls piled with potatoes, rutabaga and cabbage. The strange creatures were having a merry time, feasting, laughing and singing in awful hideous howls. Several of them had odd-looking items that turned out to be musical instruments. The creatures holding them used them to create odd, moaning sounds, and several others jumped up to sway and dance. The dancing and partying went on for hours.

Several times, Kalli saw two trolls standing near the door go outside then return. It seemed they were on guard duty.

"There are no humans outside we could see," they would shout, "and no sun is coming up yet!"

The crowd of creatures would give out a loud cheer and continue with their party. Kalli realized that like most trolls in Iceland, they would likely turn into stone if the sunlight touched them. This was helpful to him. Perhaps there was a way he could defeat them and live to tell the tale.

He waited until he thought it was close to sunrise. Gathering his courage, he took a deep breath and jumped out from his hiding place, shouting at the top of his lungs. He had grabbed the boards from the wall paneling, and holding one in each hand, he slammed them together, making a terrible racket. He bellowed, "Daybreak! Daybreak!"

The creatures were so surprised at his sudden appearance, they all started to scramble for the door, pushing and shoving each other in a confused rush. They bolted so quickly they left all their belongings. The tables, the beautiful silverware and goblets, and even the fine clothes they had discarded during the night while they were dancing littered the baðstofa.

As the monsters fled, they slipped and slid over each other, running as fast as they could, with Kalli right on their heels, chasing them. As he ran he kept slamming the panels together and shouting, "Daybreak! Daybreak!"

He chased them until they reached a lake near the farm and the creatures jumped in and vanished. Kalli realized then that they were lake-dwelling trolls, like the Nökken his Norwegian relatives had often warned him about.

The sun was coming up as he turned around to head back to the house. He saw the trolls that hadn't made it to the water, now turned into huge lumps of rough rocks strewn across the field. Kalli returned to the house. Over the next two days, he cleaned up the mess from the party, took all the silverware, clothes, and other things the trolls had left behind and made a large pile.

When the farmer arrived back home, Kalli showed him everything and told him the story of what had happened. The farmer was happy Kalli had survived the terrible night. He gave Kalli half of everything the trolls had left behind, as a reward for his bravery and quick thinking. It came to be a quite a fortune and Kalli was very pleased.

Kalli remained with the farmer several more years, and became a well-respected man. Never again were there any more strange happenings at the farm on Christmas Eve, or any other night.

DRANGEY CONSECRATED

In the early days of Iceland, there was a tiny island in the north called Drangey. No people had lived on the island in centuries, but every spring, tens of thousands of birds flocked there to nest. Drangey was halfway down one of the northern fjords called Skagafjörður (ska-ga-fyore-thur). The little island was a solid rock that had tall cliffs rising straight of the ocean and going up five hundred feet, except a small strip of shoreline on the west side of the island. There was one narrow path running from the sea to the top of the island, which was covered in thick lush grass.

One year, a group of villagers came to collect eggs from the many nests there. The group secured their boats and climbed the narrow path to the top. They separated into smaller groups and spread out across the island. In each group, some held the ropes for the ones who would climb down, and others were in charge of organizing the eggs as they were collected. They were all in good spirits, singing and laughing as they started the day.

The first group of men grabbed hold of the ropes and began to climb down the cliff to collect eggs. As the first one reached about halfway, those standing at the top heard a terrible pounding in the cliffs and several strange eerie noises. One group felt the rope they were holding shake, then sway, and suddenly break. The rope snapped and the man on the end fell down to the ocean below.

A moment later, the same thing happened to the man who had been climbing next to the first. Then, a third and a fourth had their rope break. The villagers at the top of the rock, who were holding the ropes, shouted to the remaining men to climb back up.

40

The men below saw their friends falling, and they quickly raced back up to safety.

They had no idea what had happened. The ropes were not old, and the men who fell were not inexperienced. The group gathered to look at the ropes, they saw something strange. All of the ropes were cut through as if they had been either chopped with an ax or severed with a sharp knife. There was only one explanation. They looked at each other and nodded with fear in every eye. It was clear the cliffs were inhabited by some type of being that did not want the mainlanders climbing or collecting eggs. They quickly gathered their belongings and ran down the only path which led to where the boats were anchored at the base of the cliffs.

Throughout the summer, every few weeks, a small group would go to the island to try again. Each time, the rope would be cut and the climber would fall into the ocean. No one knew how to defeat these evil trolls and, after a time, they stopped going to the island. When a famine came to the land, there was little food to eat and the villagers were desperate for the eggs they could not collect from the island.

They sent word to the Bishop Gudmundur, who had the reputation that he was not afraid of trolls and had great success in defeating trolls and all other sorts of evil spirits. He was a wonderful priest who was kind to the poor and fed them at the parish. He had sent workers to Drangey in the spring, both for fishing and bird catching, but they had not returned to the parish. The villages sent the Bishop a message that his workers had fallen prey to the trolls of the island.

After receiving the villagers' message and their plea for help, the bishop arranged a trip to Drangey with his clerics and holy water. When he came to the island, he started on the southwest side, consecrating the cliffs with holy water and prayers. He worked his way counter-clockwise, from the water's edge to the top of the cliff. For the places he couldn't climb up from the bottom, he went to the top and scaled down the rocks hanging from a rope. Slowly, he and his clerics went all around the island saying benedictions, chants, and using holy water to drive away the trolls.

He worked his way around the island and was nearly around where he started. On the Northwest side, he climbed down on a rope and started to say prayers.

When the first words were out of his mouth, a large, dirty and hairy green hand, attached to an even hairier green arm in a red sleeve, shot out from a cave in the rock. The bony hand was disfigured and held a huge, razor-sharp saber. The saber slashed out at the bishop's rope and immediately sliced through two strands of it. The arm swished through the air, jabbing and jerking.

The bishop had consecrated the rope with holy water, and no matter how hard he tried, the troll couldn't cut through the third strand. After a few minutes, the Bishop watched the hand disappear, and he heard a voice echo across the cliff wall.

"Bless no more, Bishop. The wicked need a place of their own, too."

The bishop realized the troll had a point. It wasn't their fault they were trolls, and they did need a place to live. With that, the Bishop had himself pulled up to the top of the bluff.

He gathered everyone around and declared that he would not consecrate the rest of the cliff. He was confident that they could collect eggs and would not be bothered by trolls any more.

"This part here we will leave for the trolls," he announced, with a wave of his hand. "They will no longer bother anyone who climbs anywhere else on these cliffs."

With that, they had no further troll problem and it is true to this day. No one will climb to collect eggs in the section known as Heiðnu (hay-the-na) Crag or "Pagan Crag", even though it has more birds nesting there than all the rest of the Drangey cliffs.

BJARNI SVEINSSON AND HIS SISTER SALVOR

One spring around Midsummer's night, a group of people of Skagafjörður (ska-ga-fyore-thur), in the north of Iceland, planned a trip to the mountains. Among the group was a man named Sveinn. Sveinn planned to send his son Bjarni (b'yar-knee) with the group to gather herbs and moss for medicines. When Bjarni's twin sister Salvor heard her brother was going, she insisted on going with him. They were twenty years old and had never been separated.

Sveinn didn't want his daughter to go, but she whined and begged so much that he finally agreed. But, the night before they were to leave, Sveinn had a strange dream. He dreamt he had two white birds that he loved very much. In the dream, one of the birds flew out the window and never returned.

Sveinn woke up very worried that this dream was about his children. He was convinced if he let them go on the trip, one of them would never come home. He was so afraid, he told them he would not allow either of them to go to the mountains. They argued and protested so much that Sveinn finally agreed, on the condition they keep each other in sight at all times. They both agreed and set off with their friends.

At the end of the day, the group made camp, had dinner, and went to sleep without incident. The next morning, Salvor woke up so ill that she could not get out of bed. She was too sick to travel further with the group. Bjarni remembered his promise to his father and stayed with his sister.

For three days, Salvor was ill, and every day she got sicker. Bjarni stayed with her, leaving only to collect water or hunt for food.

On the fourth day, a friend from the moss collecting group came back to check on them. Bjarni was thankful the man could stay with Salvor while he went hunting so he didn't have worry about leaving her alone. He spent some time hunting and gathering herbs, then sat down to rest next to a large boulder. He was very worried about his sister and hoped she would get better soon.

As he sat deep in though, he was interrupted by the sound of galloping horses. He looked up and saw two men on horseback heading right for him. Both were very handsome and their clothing was very fine, with ornate lining of silver, gold and jewels. One of them was dressed head-to-toe in red and was riding a red horse. The second rode a brown horse and was dressed entirely in brown. As they came up to Bjarni, they dismounted and greeted him.

"Bjarni, you look sad, tell me what is wrong," said the man in red.

"It is a private matter and you are a stranger. I would rather keep my troubles to myself," Bjarni replied.

"Every friend starts out as a stranger. I mean only to help. Please tell me your trouble."

"My sister was with me collecting moss and she became ill suddenly. It has been four days and each day she becomes weaker. I am afraid she may not survive."

"I am sorry for you are so worried, Bjarni," the man in red replied, "and I would like to help. We have a powerful healer at my home. Let me take your sister to my house that she may recover."

"No," said Bjarni, "I can't do that. I don't know who you are or where you would be taking her. Where is your home?"

"It does not matter," said the man in red. He took out a red gilded silver snuffbox with a beautiful stone inlaid in the lid.

He offered it to Bjarni and said, "Would you allow me to be guardian of your sister in exchange for this box?"

"No," said Bjarni. "I promised my father that I would stay with her no matter what and I will not break that promise. I am sorry."

"I understand," said the man, "but please keep this box as a keepsake of our chance meeting."

Bjarni then took the box and thanked him for it, thinking the man was very odd. He watched as they rode away. When he returned to his sister, the rest of the group had come back from their herb and moss gathering and had made camp around Bjarni's tent.

The following morning, the other gatherers returned to the village, but Salvor was still too ill to travel. Bjarni was worried about how sick she was, but he was also afraid the strangers he had met would come back and try to take her away. He was so afraid he couldn't sleep. He stayed awake for the whole day and night, and all of the following day.

The second night he was so tired he couldn't keep his eyes open. Still anxious she would be kidnapped, he lay down and wrapped his arms around her waist. He was sure no one could take her without waking him up. Feeling more secure, he fell into a deep and restful sleep.

In the morning he woke up and was alone. His sister was gone. Distressed, he searched all day but could not find her. Sad and feeling guilty, he returned home and told his father what had happened to them.

"The dream has come to pass," his father said. "I feared for the safety of both my children but I allowed you to go. Bjarni, I alone am to blame for the loss of your sister."

Search parties were sent out, but no trace of Salvor could be found.

Ten years passed and in time Bjarni married and took over his father's farm. One day, his shepherd came to him and said the entire flock of sheep had disappeared. He had searched for three days but could not find it.

Bjarni packed a week's worth of food and supplies and went to look for the sheep. He walked all day without rest and that night curled up in a cave to sleep.

The next morning, a heavy fog rolled in just as Bjarni started out searching. The fog was so thick he soon lost his way. He came to the edge of a large valley he had never been to before. He saw a large farmhouse and as soon as he started walking toward it, the fog instantly disappeared.

He approached a group of workers in the hayfield and asked if he might spend the night. The entire group smiled, and nodded, welcoming him warmly. He looked from one to another, each one more dazzling and beautiful than the next.

A very beautiful girl came forward and took him to the house. As they walked, Bjarni thought sadly that she looked very much like his long-lost sister.

He admired the large house and beautiful furnishings as he followed the girl to the dining room. Someone appeared and brought him food and drink and when he was full, he was led to a small sleeping room where he immediately fell into bed and was soon fast asleep.

He awoke the next morning well-rested. He could hear laughter and singing coming from another part of the house and one voice, louder than the others, sounded familiar to him. He shook his head, certain his imagination was getting the better of him. First, he thought a young girl looked like his sister, now he thought an unseen singer sounded like his sister. He got up and opened the door, finding fresh clothes lying in the hallway. As he was getting dressed, there was a knock on the door.

Opening it, Bjarni saw a small boy standing there.

"Well, good morning there my lad," he said.

"Good morning," the boy replied, "I heard we had a visitor and wanted to meet you."

"Well, it is nice to meet you. I am Bjarni."

"Come – I will take you to breakfast," the boy said.

Bjarni followed the boy and walked into a large dining room with a table full of people. As he looked around, to his surprise, Bjarni saw the man in red that he had met years before when his sister disappeared. At the other end of the table, he recognized the second rider that day, the one in brown. Bjarni was shocked to see his long-lost sister there in the center, dressed in riches and looking very healthy. She met his eyes, and he knew instantly she recognized him as well. She smiled, and had tears of happiness in her eyes. She got up from the table and ran to him, hugging him tightly.

"I was so sad when I lost you but I am so happy to see you again my brother."

They sat down to breakfast and Bjarni told his sister everything that had happened in Skagafjörður since she left. Asking what happened to her, she turned to the man in red, who told Bjarni the story.

"I took your sister from you, Bjarni, for she surely would have died of her illness. I brought her here and once she recovered, she married my son. I took your sheep and made it so you would find you way here so the two of you could see each other again.

47

Tomorrow, I will return your flock, but tonight, stay here and talk to your sister."

They spent all night catching up and in the morning bid each other a tearful goodbye. Bjarni went with the man in red and his sister's husband to collect Bjarni's herd of sheep. Bjarni got to know both men during the trip, and liked them both very much.

He realized now that they were not ordinary people, but part of the Hidden Folk. He thought his sister was very lucky to have married into such a good family. Because of this, he was very pleased when the man in red offered for Bjarni and his family to move to the valley and live with them.

In the spring, they came back to lead Bjarni's entire family and all their livestock to the secret valley, where they lived a long time. In his old age, he returned to Skagafjörður and shared this story of his sister and the mysterious valley.

THE SEALSKIN

There once was a man named Unnar who lived in the southern town of Vik. One morning, he was walking on the beach, between the water's edge and the towering cliff. It was very early, when the sun was just starting to peek over the horizon. As he walked, he came across a cave where he heard sounds of music and laughter, as if a great party were taking place.

He drew closer and saw a huge pile of sealskins lying at the mouth of the cave. Looking around, Unnar quickly grabbed one of the skins, and then rushed home. He knew the owner of the sealskin would not be able to return to the sea without it. The creature would be caught in human form, completely dependent on the goodwill of others. Knowing all this, Unnar carefully wrapped the skin in several furs, then placed it at the bottom of a trunk and locked the trunk.

He spent the day tending his livestock and doing his chores on the farm. With his work done, he walked back to the ocean and checked the cave he had found that morning. As he approached, he heard the sound of crying. He found a beautiful woman, wrapped in a plain cloak, sobbing. He knew this was the seal whose skin he had taken, but he pretended to know nothing.

"What's wrong, why are you sad?" he asked her, wondering what she might say.

"I have lost something very valuable and cannot return home without it," she sobbed.

"Is there something I can do? Can I help you look?" Unnar was uncomfortable, feeling bad that he had caused her so much unhappiness.

"No, it is of no use," she sighed, "I don't know what I will ever do now."

"Come with me," he said, "I will give you a place to stay. In return, you can cook or keep house for me, if you have the skills."

"Thank you very much. I am not sure I can, but perhaps you can teach me. I am most grateful for a place to stay." She jumped up and together they crossed the beach and climbed the cliffs toward Unnar's farm.

She stayed with him for many months and in time they became quite fond of each other. She would never tell him her name, so he called her Arun, like "ah-roon" which meant *Secret*. Arun loved Unnar in her own way, but she was very distant and quiet around other people. When her housework was done, she would often just sit and gaze out at the sea for hours.

In time, they married and had several children. They led a quiet and content life. Unnar spent long hours working the farm and tending to the herd of sheep, often leaving Arun and the children alone. He was careful to keep the sealskin locked away and kept the key on a length of cord around his neck.

One day, he realized the cord and they key were gone. Thinking the cord must have frayed and broken, Unnar searched the farm. He looked high and low, through the barn, the house, the smithy, the hayfield and his fishing boat.

While Unnar searched for the missing key, Arun had finished her housework and, as she often did, sat staring wistfully at the sea. As she sat, her youngest son came running up to her, struggling with a large bundle.

"Mama! Mama! Look what I found," he shouted at her.

Arun turned and her heart skipped a beat. Her child held her beloved sealskin. Barely able to contain her excitement, she said, "My, what a treasure you have. Where did you find such a thing?"

"I found a key and the only lock I have ever seen is the trunk stored in the loft. I found this under a pile of furs. Isn't it beautiful?"

"Yes, my son, it is quite lovely," Arun said.

"You should have it, mama, because it is as beautiful as you are," the boy said sincerely.

With tears in her eyes, Arun replied, "Thank you, dear boy, thank you so very much."

Her heart was breaking. She belonged in the sea, but she loved her husband and children very much.

> *This I want, and yet I want it not, --*
> *I struggle between what I once had and now have got*
> *On land have I seven children, six sons and a daughter,*
> *But seven more children have I in my home in the water.*
> *Of two minds must I be*
> *My loves of both the farm and the sea.*

The call of the water was too strong. Arun hugged her children goodbye and tried to explain why she was leaving and where she was going. They didn't understand she was actually a seal and belonged in the ocean. She showed them the skin and with tears in her eyes, she put it on. As they watched, she changed into a seal and jumped into the sea.

Unnar came home and was miserable without her, but he knew her true home was the ocean. He would watch for her when he was out in his boat. He knew that the sad-looking seal circling his craft was her. If he fished, his nets were always full. Even when others had back luck, Unnar never came back without catching fish.

Sometimes, when he would walk along the shoreline with their children, a seal swam offshore, keeping pace with them. They would find pretty shells and brightly colored fish thrown on the shore in front of them and knew they were gifts from her. But never again did their mother return to the land.

HALLGERÐUR OF BLAFELL

There once was a man named Olafur who was from Eyjafjörður (aye-ya-fyore-thur). Every year, he went south to Stafnes to work as a fisherman.

One year, as Olafur was headed across the mountains, it began to snow. It snowed so hard, he could not see and soon was lost. He was very cold and searched for a cave or shelter where he could pass the night safely, but he could not find any shelter. The snow didn't stop and he soon had no idea what direction he was walking.

After a while, he saw a large shape in front of him and he recognized it as the mountain Blafell. He was relieved to know where he was. As he walked closer, he saw an enormous trollwife just ahead of him.

She saw him through the snow and challenged him. Olafur was afraid because trolls were known to be ill-tempered and unpredictable. The troll wife said to him,

You there human, you ride here so assured
Do you not know I am the troll called Hallgerður (halt-geth-thur)
I will instill a fear so future travel be deterred
My frightful reputation will be assured
If I make a wicked death for you occur
Unless you tell me why on this path you were

Olafur didn't argue with the trollwife or give her any reason for his travel. He had learned that the best way to deal with an angry troll, or person for that matter, was to be kind. He replied to her in a jolly voice:

"Hail to you and hearty greetings, Hallgerður of Blafell."

The trollwife was quite surprised at the friendly greeting, and immediately her mood improved.

He called back to him, "Few have ever addressed me so sweetly, you may pass and go in peace, my dearest dear."

Olafur was relieved and followed the trail through the mountains. He saw the trollwife's tracks in the snow as he traveled. Looking down, he noticed there seemed to be spots of blood in them.

He called to her, "Are you injured Hallgerður of Blafell?"

He stopped the packhorse he was leading and offered her a seat on his back.

"You may ride this packhorse I have, if you promise not to hurt him."

She accepted gratefully and said, "Pain's felt by all, even the troll."

She and Olafur rode for a while in silence until they came to a fork in the road. Olafur now knew where he was and could continue his journey to Stafnes. The trollwife turned to follow a different path but wished him well for the rest of his trip.

"Thank you Olafur for your kind help. When you arrive at Stafnes, turn your horses loose and do not worry anymore about them."

Olafur's journey went smoothly from then on. When he reached Stafnes, he turned the horses loose as the trollwife had directed and they soon disappeared.

He had a good fishing season and in the spring when he was ready to head north the horses returned. They were fat and well-groomed. Olafur went back north, and lived an uneventful life.

THE SERPENT OF LAGARFLJÓT

In the early days of Iceland, a long, long time ago, there was a woman who lived on a small farm with her daughter, Rin. The farm was near Lake Lagarfljot, close to where the lake is fed by a small stream. On Rin's sixteenth birthday, her mother gave her a gold ring.

Rin said to her, "Mother, how can I make the most out of this gold?"

"Put it under a ling snake," said the woman. It was common in Iceland to use a ling snake, or Heath-Dragon, as they were also called, to nurture gold. The magical creature would grow bigger and bigger as long as it was kept on gold. In turn, the amount of gold would grow along with the Heath-Dragon.

Rin followed her mother's advice and set out to capture the dragon. She easily caught a small one and tucked it into her linen chest with the gold ring at the bottom. Feeling that she had followed her mother's instructions, Rin promptly forgot about the ring and the tiny Heath-Dragon. She spent her days working hard on the farm, tending to the animals and helping her mother with the housework. They had field hands to feed, sheep to tend, and hayfields to mow.

Weeks passed before Rin thought about the ring and the little dragon. She went to the closet and lifted the lid of the chest, pleased to see the dragon was nearly three times the size it had been when she first caught it. She could see that the gold had grown as well. She reached in, but pulled her hand back when the growing dragon hissed and snapped at her. She slammed the lid of the chest shut and locked it.

Rin was worried about how big the Heath-Dragon might get and how dangerous it might be. At dinner that night, Rin asked her mother for advice on the growing dragon in the chest.

"I don't know if the chest is big enough or the dragon is happy. How do I know if it's dangerous or what if he grows too big and is smothered in the box?"

"When I was young, I kept a Heath-Dragon for several years in a small chest. He grew a small amount of gold into a very sizeable amount. The chest held him and the gold quite nicely."

"Years?" Rin said, surprised. "It was really alright?"

"I don't know that I've heard of one growing too large. I'm sure it is quite fine," her mother said calmly.

With her mother's soothing words, Rin's concern quickly left her mind. Weeks passed again before she again thought of the gold.

This time, when she checked in the closet, the Heath-Dragon had grown so large that the chest was beginning to split at the seams. This was no normal dragon and Rin was very afraid. If it continued to grow at this rate, it would soon split the house!

She quickly hitched a horse to their small cart they used for market. She wrapped the broken chest in a length of linen and used the material to drag it across the floor and out the door. She called to one of the hired men, who lifted the heavy chest into the cart for her. She refused his offer to accompany her, not wanting anyone to know about the growing monster she carried in the cart.

Not knowing what else to do, she drove the cart down to the lake's edge, and pushed the chest until it fell off the cart and tumbled into the water. Relieved, she jumped in the cart and quickly headed back home without a backwards glance.

She did not see the head of a sea monster above the water that watched her. As soon as she was out of sight, the dragon-like creature swam over and retrieved the Heath-Dragon and the gold.

Rin could not have known that the creature watching her was a descendent of the Icelandic Guardian Dragon and that this was his lake to protect. Now, the little Heath Dragon and the gold were his to protect as well.

Rin stayed busy for the next couple of months, not giving a thought to the Heath-Dragon or the gold that now lay at the bottom of Lake Lagarfljot. One day, she overheard two field hands talking.

"It's a menace, I tell you," said the first one.

"Yow, something must be done, and soon," replied the other. "None of us, man or beast, will soon be safe from that monster."

"Jonas heard that the serpent came right up on land, spitting venom and ate up three sheep in just one bite!"

Rin listened and was certain the serpent they spoke of was the Heath-Dragon she had thrown into the lake. How could such a thing have happened? People were being terrorized and livestock eaten by a monster she created. She quickly ran to the house and confessed everything to her mother. Her mother was wise in many things and knew exactly what to do.

She immediately sent for two Sami warriors from Finland. They were fierce Viking warriors and were known to be the most skilled at battling sea monsters. The fastest ship in the land was sent to bring them back to Lake Lagarfljot.

The Sami warriors arrived within weeks, to the great relief of everyone that lived around the lake. The warriors dove into the lake and quickly found the serpent. They used their great strength and fought long and hard against the beast.

The battle raged and the Finns finally managed to secure the beast. When they came out of the water, they shared what they had found.

There was not just one Heath-Dragon in the lake, but two. One was under the gold and the other above it. The two together were fiercer than any other monster the Finns had ever battled.

"There is no doubt the larger of the two is descendent from the Icelandic Guardian, the Dragon," one of the Sami proclaimed. "That beast is protective of the smaller dragon, and they both protect the gold."

They could not kill them, they were too strong. Neither could they recover the gold with both dragons protecting it. The best the Finns were able to do was chain both serpents down. This would keep them from coming out of the water.

Today, the Heath-Dragon can still be seen moving about in the lake. It grew in mystery because it was always seen just before a natural disaster, like a volcanic eruption. Because it is chained, all that can be seen are one or two humps, making it look a bit like an oversized worm.

In time, people forgot about Rin's dragon and the mysterious lake beast became known as the Monster Worm.

THE STORY OF PRINCE HLINI

In the early days of Iceland, there was a powerful Viking Chieftain named Hringur who ruled over a very large territory. He and his wife had a son named Hlini, that they often called their little Prince Hlini.

From the time he was a boy, Hlini was strong, handsome, smart, and kind to his family and everyone in the territory. He worked hard at his studies, becoming accomplished in his schoolwork and all the skills needed to be a good Viking. He learned to hunt and fish, he handled a broadsword expertly and was very skillful with his bow and arrow by the time he was twenty.

Hlini would often lead his father's men on hunting parties. During one of these trips, just as they finished their hunt and were preparing to return home, a heavy fog suddenly surrounded them. It was so thick that soon one man could not see the man next to him. They walked carefully toward each other's voices, touching shoulder to shoulder to keep from getting lost. Looking around, they realized that Hlini was not in the group.

The men used ropes to tie themselves together so they would not get separated while they searched for Prince Hlini. They called his name and searched the mountainside through the trees and thick brush. They searched through caves, crevices and rocky outcroppings but could not find him anywhere.

Finally, the fog became less and they could see a little better, but the darkness of night came quickly and stopped their search. The next day, they searched from dawn to dusk but no trace of Hlini could be found.

The men had no choice but to return to Chief Hringur and tell him his son had been lost. The Chieftain was very sad, but was certain his son was alive. Hlini was healthy and strong, and he was a very good hunter so he would not go hungry. Chief Hringur thought he simply was separated from his horse and would find his way back on his own. To be sure, he organized another group of men to go find his son to bring him home.

After a week, the second group returned to Chief Hringur with the news that they had found no trace of Hlini. The Chieftain was very worried about his son but would not give up hope. He issued a plea to his entire realm for help in finding his son. The Chieftain promised whoever could bring the boy home would be rewarded with half of all the lands he owned and half his livestock.

One of the field hands heard the Chieftain's request and told his family the story over dinner that night. His daughter, Signy, was very smart and had been taught many Viking skills. She was skilled with bow and arrow, was quick with her sword, and accomplished in hunting, sailing, navigation.

"Father," she said, "I would like to help our Chieftain and go find Hlini."

"You are well-suited for the task, Signy," he replied, "You are brave and generous and I am proud of you that you would accept this dangerous task."

Having her father's blessing, Signy set off the next morning to search for the prince. She walked for hours, from sunrise until late in the afternoon. She followed the path to where the men had first lost sight of Hlini and there she started searching for clues. For many hours she carefully walked and searched until she found the clue she sought. She saw a slight glimmer and heard the faint sound of voices and music, like a party in the distance.

"Hidden Folks, I need your help," she called into the empty air. "Prince Hlini has been taken from his family and I need your aid to find him."

Signy knew the Hidden Ones would help. They were the protectors of Iceland, the land and the good people who cared for the land as much as they did. She might not be able to see the Hidden, but she trusted them.

After a very short time, she saw a glimmer of light, something shimmering ahead in the brush. She walked towards the spot, then saw another glimmer, further away. The lights seemed to be leading her, so she followed. A few hours later, the shimmering stopped and Signy looked around. In the rocks above her, she saw an opening of a cave. Carefully, she climbed up to take a look inside.

As she snuck inside, moving slowly and quietly along the wall of the cave, she quickly saw that the cave was very big and had many pieces of very large, elaborate furniture. In one corner were two huge beds. The first was made of pure silver, the second made of gold. Signy looked closer and saw the prince lying sound asleep in the gold bed.

There were symbols carved at the centers of each of the headboards, and Signy recognized them as Viking runic characters. Large graceful swans were carved at either end of the headboards. Suddenly, there was a loud shuffling and thumping coming from the cave entrance.

"*Why isn't Hlini waking up?*" Signy wondered as she scrambled to hide in the shadows of the cave wall.

She barely managed to hide herself when two large, ugly-looking giantesses entered the cave. One of them had white-blonde hair and a huge pointy nose and the other had dark hair and large warts on the end of her square chin.

As they came inside, the blond one stopped, sniffed, and said, "Fy, fo, someone has been here! Our cave smells like humans."

"Pfftt, sister – it is just the scent of Price Hlini," the wart-covered one replied calmly, as her sister lumbered over to the beds.

Standing at the foot of the gold bed, she chanted, "Sing, my swans, sing sweetly and my Prince Hlini shall wake".

Signy watched in astonishment and she heard the swans sing and Hlini woke up. He immediately jumped to his feet and glared at the giantess.

The blonde giantess looked at him adoringly, seeming not to notice his anger. She asked him sweetly, "Hlini are you hungry? Would you like some food?"

"No," he answered and he tried to jump from the bed. The giantess caught him easily and returned him to the small prison.

"Hlini will you marry me?" she asked, as if nothing had happened.

"No. As I have said every day before this, no, I will not."

The blonde giantess looked sad, shaking her head as she chanted, "Sing, my swans, sing sweetly and my Prince Hlini shall sleep".

They sang, and he immediately went back to sleep. The blonde giantess walked to the other side of the room. Signy watched as the two giantesses prepared and ate their dinner. They both laid down in the silver bed and were soon snoring loudly. Signy crept under the safety of the gold bed where she curled up and fell asleep.

The next morning, Signy watched from under the bed as the giantesses started their day.

As she had the night before, the giantess stood at the foot of the gold bed and chanted, "Sing, my swans, sing sweetly and my Prince Hlini shall wake".

The swans sang, and Hlini woke up and lunged for the floor. The giantess was prepared for his sudden movement and caught him before he could bolt for freedom.

Holding on to one foot as he glared at her, she asked, "Hlini are you hungry? Would you like some food?"

"No" he answered, refusing to look at her.

"Hlini will you marry me?" she asked.

"No."

The giantess simply smiled and chanted for the swans to sing Hlini to sleep. This done, she and her sister left.

When she felt it was safe, Signy crept out from under the bed and walked quietly to the cave entrance. She looked around outside to make sure the giantesses were gone. Feeling confident, she ran over to Price Hlini and repeated the chant she had heard the giantess use.

"Sing, my swans, sing sweetly and my Prince Hlini shall wake".

Hlini woke up and immediately jumped to the floor and quickly scanned the room. Neither giantess was in sight. He looked at Signy, confused.

"Hlini, my name is Signy," she said. "Your father and many men have been searching for you. The Hidden helped lead me here to find you. Are you injured?"

"No," he replied, "how long have I been here?"

"A week," she said, "maybe a bit more. What happened?"

He told her the story of how he had been separated from his men and how he came across the cave with the giantesses. He had been trapped ever since and the sleeping spell made it impossible for him to form an escape plan.

"We should leave now," he said, jumping from the bed.

"Wait, we should consider this. Why are they holding you here and why do you think the giantess wants you to marry her?" Signy wondered.

"I don't know, but that is a good question," he said thoughtfully. "I don't want them to come to the village after us. We need to destroy them here."

Signy told him everything she had learned by watching the two sisters. Hlini said they needed to think on the problem some and come up with a plan.

Signy suggested, "You should tell that ugly giantess you will marry her if she tells you what the runes on the beds mean and what she and her sister do all day. Maybe she will tell you something that will help."

The prince agreed it would be a good idea to know more about the giantesses and that the information might help them defeat the sisters. That decided, they talked of all kinds of things. As they talked, they played chess to pass the time. The afternoon wore on and Hlini asked Signy to say the chant and put him to sleep. He didn't want to risk the giantesses coming home when he was still awake. Signy did as he asked and then she crept back to her hiding place against the wall.

When the two giantesses came in the cave, they set about making dinner and did not notice anything amiss. When the food was ready, the wart-faced one spoke the chant to awaken Hlini.

"Hlini are you hungry? Would you like some food?"

"Yes, thank you," he replied. She happily filled a bowl with a rich stew and brought it to him.

"Hlini will you marry me?" she asked when he had finished.

"Yes, I will, on one condition," Hlini said.

"I see. What is your condition?" the giantess said, suspicious.

"Tell me what these rune carvings on the beds mean."

The giantess thought for a moment and decided there could be no harm in telling him what he wanted to know.

"They are spells that allow me to use magic," she said. "This one here," she said as she pointed, "means 'Fly, Fly, oh bed of mine; to that place I see in my mind's eye' and I can fly to any point in the world I can imagine."

"That must be so fun," he said. "What do you and your sister do all day?"

"Oh, we hunt some, humans if we can find some, or other meat if there are no humans to hunt. When the afternoon is warm, we like to find a shady spot and play catch with our life egg."

Hlini knew that a giant must carry their life force, called a life egg, with them wherever they went. They had to be very careful because if it broke, the giant would die.

"You only have one?" he asked her.

"Yes," she replied, "my sister and I are twins and share a life egg. Neither of us will give it up, but since we both want to hold it, we often play catch."

"Thank you for telling me these things," he told her, "I am tired now and would like to rest."

The giantess said goodnight and used the chant to put him under the sleeping spell. In the morning, she woke Hlini and shared breakfast with him. She asked if he would join them in the woods for the day. He said no, and that he preferred to stay home. To that, she said goodbye and again used the chant to put him to sleep.

After the giantesses had left, Signy used the same chant to wake Hlini. "We should sneak up on the giantesses when they are under the shade tree," she said, "When they start to bring out their life egg, you can throw your spear at it and destroy it."

The prince agreed, and then grabbed her hand and pulled her up so that she stood by him on the bed. Together, they chanted, "Fly, Fly, oh bed of mine - out to the woods where the twin giantesses play."

The whole bed flew out the cave entrance and soared over the valley, slowing down when they reached the shade trees at the edge of the woods. They heard the voices of the two giantesses, laughing and playing with the egg.

Signy motioned up towards the trees and Hlini quickly climbed the tree to be directly above the two sisters. As one tossed the life

egg to the other, Hlini threw his spear. His aim was true and it struck the egg in the center, breaking it into hundreds of small pieces. Both giantesses shrieked and fell over dead.

They returned to the cave and loaded all the gold, silver and the rest of the giantesses' treasure onto the beds. Hlini gave the treasure to Signy's parents so they would be comfortable for the rest of their lives.

Hlini and Signy went to the palace and the Chieftain was very happy to have his son back safe. Hlini told his father everything that happened to him. He told the story exactly the way it was written here. The Chieftain thanked Signy for saving his son's life and offered her any reward she could name.

"I wish to remain with your son," she said, looking at Hlini with love.

Hlini asked his father's permission to marry her and the king agreed.

The Prince and Signy grew to love each other very much and were happy for many years. And so ends this story.

DEEP CHANNELS

There was a certain trollwife who lived in Norway. She had friends who had moved to Iceland and she wanted to go for a visit. From Norway to Iceland was a day's walk for the trollwife, as she was quite large and with one step she could go a very long distance.

One day she sat with another trollwife, discussing her plans.

"No, no, you don't want to wade that. I hear there are deep channels along the way," her friend said, shaking her head.

"Yes, I have heard the Iceland channels are deep, but I think they are fordable," she said. "Although, I do believe there is one narrow trench near the middle of the ocean that is so deep it might be over my head and I'm afraid I may get my hair wet."

Still determined, she set off a few days later and started wading toward Iceland. It was later in the afternoon when she reached the channel she was afraid was too deep. She stuck her foot out, trying to feel for the ocean floor.

Just then, a large whale swam by, tickling the bottom of her foot. She jerked back and stumbled. She flapped her arms, causing huge waves to ripple from the coast of Iceland clear to the shores of Norway and Scotland.

A large ship was passing by and the trollwife grabbed for it, intending to use it as support. The ship's captain had seen the huge troll and worked frantically to stay just out of her reach. She stretched as far as she could, but couldn't reach the ship. The effort put her more off balance and she fell headfirst into the trench where she drowned.

Her body later washed ashore, in the Western Fjords at Rauðisandur (Ray-the-saunder). She was turned to rock from the sun and lay flat on her back with her feet and toes sticking straight up. She was so large that a man on horseback could ride at the water's edge and be in the shadow of her massive feet.

THE MAKING OF DRANGEY

In the early days of Iceland there were very few people, but many trolls. They made their homes in the mountains, the deep ravines, and along the rocky shoreline of the ocean. But, wherever they chose to make their home, they were all careful to avoid the sunlight. Nearly all trolls are deathly allergic to sunlight. If a troll is caught out in the sunlight, it will immediately turn to stone.

Iceland is so very far north, it is near the Arctic Circle and the sun shines differently there. During the wintertime, the sun only shines for four or five hours a day. But, in the summer, the sun shines for twenty hours. Trolls can only safely be outside for three or four hours each day.

On the north side of Iceland was an odd old troll. He and his trollwife lived on the banks of Skagafjörður (skag-a-fyore-thur) on the side that was called Tröllaskagi (trud-la-sky-ye), or Troll Peninsula.

The couple had a cow they wanted to breed, but the only bull was on the other side of the fjord. To walk the land all the way around would take too many hours. Since it was summertime, the sun would only set for a few hours each day. Their only choice was to walk across the fjord, through the water, to the other side.

So, they made their preparation to go as quickly as possible.

At sunset, they started wading across the fjord. The old troll grabbed the cow's rope and pulled from the front and his wife pushed it from the rear. The cow snorted and tried to back up. The

troll and his wife grunted and groaned until they got the cow moving. Slowly, they started to wade across the fjord.

The cow pulled her head away from the rope, and swished her tail in the wife's face. This was a very stubborn cow. At one point, she sat down on a rock in the middle of the fjord, refusing to go any further.

The trolls decided they would need to dive down under the water and lift the cow between them. If they balanced the cow on their shoulders, they could swim to the other side. This worked much better than pushing and pulling the stubborn cow.

It still took longer than they planned to reach the other side of the fjord. The cow wiggled and bellowed. The ground underwater was uneven and they both stumbled often. They had trouble gauging the sunlight because their heads were underwater from the weight of the cow on their shoulders. Every so often, one would poke their head up and check for sunrise.

About the third time the lead troll checked, he saw the golden glow of the sun rising in the east. He quickly tried to get his huge feet under his body so he could stand up in the fjord. Reaching under the water, he swept his arm back and forth to get his wife's attention and warn her.

But it was too late. Just as she stood up to see what he needed, the troll saw the bright rays of sunshine pouring over the horizon. He stood at the head of their cow, the wife at the tail and the cow in between them. All three froze into solid rock. The poor cow turned to stone only because the trolls were touching her.

In this way, the cow became the island of Drangey, and the troll and his troll wife each became giant rock pillars on either side of the island. One fell apart in a huge earthquake a hundred years ago but the other still stands today.

TROLLS OF THE WEST FJORDS

There once were three horrible trolls that lived in the far northwest of Iceland, in an area known as the Western Fjords. They were named Kerling, Bitru, and Koll. The trio was very troublesome and loved to disrupt the travels of humans. They caused landslides, stole luggage, and scared the horses so that they bolted away. The three became such a problem that the people from the villages in the area came together to find a solution.

First, they begged the Hidden Folk to talk to the trolls and make peace. The Hidden Folk would not help because they valued the land above everything else. Kerling, Bitru and Koll were not harming the land, they were only a problem for the humans. This did not bother the Hidden Folks very much and they told the villagers to solve the problem themselves.

The villagers held a council to talk about what they could do about the problem. The meeting lasted for hours and they talked long into the night. Bitru snuck close and hid in the rocks near the meeting tent. He listened to every word with his keen troll ears. He eavesdropped as they talked and made their plans to rid themselves of the trolls. After many ideas were thrown out and rejected, the council decided to call for the Viking warriors to come battle the trolls. They hoped the warriors could drive them away. Bitru heard every word of their plan and quickly ran back to Kerling and Koll to tell them what he had heard.

"We must leave before the warriors arrive," Koll insisted, "They will surely kill us."

"No, we are trolls and this is our home, we must fight!" shouted Kerling.

Bitru thoughtfully tapped his huge troll finger against one of the many warts that covered his face. "What if the warriors could not come here to fight?" he said slowly.

"What do you mean? Why wouldn't they come?" Koll demanded.

Bitru sneered in his troll-version of a smile. "Not WOULD, I said COULD."

Bitru took a stick and drew a rough map in the dirt. "We need a safe place to live where we won't be bothered by humans trying to drive us away. But, this is our home, right here."

"Yes, yes," agreed Koll and Kerling together, staring at the ground.

"We dig a trench and let the ocean divide the land here," he drew another line in the dirt. "This will make the Western Fjords an island. If it is separate from Iceland, they could not send their warriors without using boats."

"And boats we can sink!" cried Koll joyfully.

"We couldn't dig that soon enough. It will take too long," Kerling argued.

"Bah! I challenge you, Kerling. Use your troll strength. Koll and I will dig from the south and you dig from the north."

They stared at each other before Bitru continued. "If we meet in the middle, we all share the new island. If we dig more, you will take the land we choose to give you."

"And if we don't finish at all before the warriors arrive?" she said doubtfully.

"Then we may be driven to Greenland," Bitru said sadly. They all looked at each other. None of them wanted to live in Greenland. It was snowy and cold all the time, and there were no humans to play tricks on. And, there weren't very many boats to have fun sinking.

So, they all agreed to Bitru's plan. Bitru and Koll started digging a channel from Breiðafjörður (braith–a–fyore–thur) on the Atlantic Ocean side, digging northeast. Kerling started from the north, in the Húnaflói (huna–flowy) fjord. Kerling used her ox and fastened a harness so that the animal could walk along and drag a scoop to dig a

channel. As the ox walked, Kerling followed with her shovel, digging frantically to make a deep trench. It quickly filled in with water.

Bitru and Koll were very strong and worked quickly, cutting a huge gap in the land. Unfortunately for them, it was summertime and the night lasted only a few hours. They dug as quickly as they could, and, in time, they could see Kerling and her ox in the distance.

They dug faster, encouraging each other with the happy thoughts of a new island all to themselves. If they dug fast enough, they would give only the smallest northern part to KIerling, the part few people lived and even few boats passed. They drew closer.

"Ho, there!" They called to her.

She turned, and became very angry that they were so close.

"It is not fair," she shouted, "the two of you are faster together than me and my ox."

She realized she was not going to finish her task of meeting them halfway. They would have a bigger share of the island and she would be left to only a small part.

She began to hack at the land with her shovel, making a choppy mess of the coastline. She was desperate to come up with a way to have half of the island. Intent on her work, she didn't notice the first rays of the sun coming up over the horizon.

Bitru and Koll didn't notice the sunrise either. They were determined to beat Kerling and were shoveling so fast that huge chunks of dirt and rocks were flying into the fjord, creating many tiny islands in the water.

Kerling looked up and saw how close they were. In a rage, she slammed her shovel down into the cliffs and a huge section broke off.

It went flying into Steingrímsfjörður (stain-greems-fyore-thur) bay north of her and formed the island Grimsey.

Bitru and Koll realized too late that the sun was peeking over the horizon. They tried to hide from the sun in shadows of the cliffs but they were too slow. The sun rose, they turned to stone.

Kerling saw her friends turn to rock and tried to save herself by jumping over the fjord. She scrambled along the cliffs to stay out of the early morning sun. Her ox had continue walking and Kerling ran to catch up, thinking she could hide in the ox's shadow. As fast as she ran, wasn't quick enough either.

Like Bitru and Koll, she turned to stone. Today, all that is left of her is the profile of her face, watching over Grimsey Island from the coastal town of Drangsnes.

THE GHOST AND THE CASHBOX

In the north of Iceland, there once lived a man who was as rich as he was stingy. He had great wealth but hated to part with his money. Everyone in the land knew hoarded his immense wealth. His wife, Silfra, was the opposite of her husband, being very kind and generous. She constantly worked to help others, but try as she might, she could not convince her husband to change his selfish ways.

One winter he became very sick and died. After his burial, his affairs were set in order. To everyone's surprise, there was no cash to be found. Even his poor widow had no idea where the money was, and they spent days searching the farm and the grounds. Shortly after he was buried, strange things started to happen. There were odd lights and sounds coming from the graveyard. Any time someone searched the house for the money, there were loud noises and shadowy figure following the searcher.

It was soon clear that the farm was haunted and everyone was sure it was Silfra's husband returning to be near his money. Throughout the winter the haunting grew worse, and as the spring came, people prepared to leave the troubled place. Even Silfra was ready to give up the farm and find a new place to live.

This went on until the early summer, at a time known in Iceland as Moving Days, which was around the end of May. This was the time when farm workers would change jobs, moving from one farm to another. It was common at this time for new workers to arrive seeking a job.

It was during Moving Days that a field hand named Tindar came to Silfra, looking for a job. Because so many people had left, she hired him immediately. After only a few days, he discovered the farm was haunted and he asked her about it.

"Was your husband a wealthy man?" Tindar asked her. "Did he have a large fortune?"

"We all thought so, but after he died, we never found any money," she answered. "If he had a fortune, he hid it well."

Throughout the summer the haunting continued. Market time arrived in the fall, when farmers took their wares into town and everyone went shopping. Tindar went to help with the wares, hoping there would be time when he could do some errands of his own.

The work went quickly and Tindar had time for his shopping. He bought large sheets of tin and several yards of white linen. When he returned to the farm, Tindar had a long cloak sewn from the linen. He was a skilled metal worker so he took the tin sheets and made a metal breastplate and gloves for himself.

His preparations complete, he waited for a dark night. When it came, he waited for everyone else to go to sleep. Tindar put on his breastplate and the metal gloves, then put on the white cloak. Satisfied, he tiptoed to the church graveyard, and began to walk near the grave of Silfa's husband. As he paced back and forth, he flipped a shiny silver coin.

Soon, Tindar saw a ghost rise from the grave. The ghost looked right at Tindar, scowling.

"Have you passed on? You're one of us?" he said suspiciously.

"Yes, I am quite dead," replied Tindar.

"Let me feel your hand to see if you are warm," said the ghost.

Tindar held out his hand and the ghost felt the metal and found it was cold.

"Yes, you're a ghost all right," he said. "Why have you returned?"

"To play with my silver piece," said Tindar.

"Just the one coin?" exclaimed the ghost, shaking his head. "That hardly seems worth it. What if I told you I had much more?"

"You have a lot of coins?" Tindar asked.

"Yes I do!" said the ghost, happily, "I'll show you"

Tindar ran quickly after the ghost as they left the graveyard and went to edge of the homefield. The ghost stopped and motioned for Tindar to turn his back, trying to keep his hiding place a secret. Tindar pretended to turn away and cover his eyes, but he was sneaky and watched through his fingers the whole time. Tindar saw the ghost kick at a hummock, revealing a dirty cashbox. When he opened it, he dumped out a large pile of silver coins onto the ground.

The two of them sat and played with the money most of the night, stacking it and tossing it, and even trying to juggle some of them. Mostly, they just sat admiring the shine of each silver piece in the moonlight.

"We must put this away now, the dawn is coming," said the ghost.

"Soon, soon, I haven't played with the small ones yet," Tindar replied.

As the ghost tried to gather the silver, Tindar would scatter them again.

The ghost became frustrated and said, "You are no ghost."

"Of course I am," Tindar scoffed, "Feel the coldness of my hand." He stretched out his hand to the ghost again.

"Yes, it's cold," he admitted as he reached for the coins, grabbing and dropping them in the box. There were a few he couldn't reach and Tindar grabbed those and threw them in the air. At this, the ghost got very angry.

"You cannot be a ghost, you must be very much alive, and are trying to steal my silver!" he accused Tindar.

"No, I would not!" Tindar cried as the ghost grabbed him by the chest.

Again, the ghost felt the cold and admitted, "It must be true that you and I are both ghosts, your body is cold as the grave."

Again he started gathering up the silver pieces and Tindar helped him put the coins in the box.

"I'm going to put my silver piece in with your money," he said.

"Yes, that is fine with me," said the ghost. He put the box back, piling dirt around it and placing the hummock on top. The hiding place secure, they headed back to the graveyard by the church.

"Where is your gravesite?" asked the ghost.

"On the other side," Tindar said, waving vaguely.

The steward stood still. "I'll wait for you to go first," he said.

"No," Tindar replied, "You can go first."

The sun was starting to come up as they argued. Tindar wouldn't move and finally the ghost had to jump into his grave as the first rays of sunlight came over the hill.

Tindar immediately ran back to the homefield and dug the

cashbox out from under the hummock. He knew the ghost smell of the earth was strong and the man's ghost would be able to find the cashbox by sniffing. He had to make sure the ghost couldn't sniff it out.

He returned to the farmhouse and found a large wine cask, which he filled with water. He placed the cashbox in the cask of water, and for good measure, hid his ghost outfit inside as well.

That night, after everyone went to bed, the ghost rose from the graveyard and immediately headed for the hummock and his box of coins. His roar of anger could be heard throughout the valley when he discovered the cashbox was missing. He searched the barn and then the house. Tindar was sleeping just inside the door and woke up as the ghost searched the house, sniffing for his lost silver. He sniffed and searched in all directions but never found the coins.

When daybreak was near, the ghost had to abandon his search and return to his grave. Tindar followed him, and sealed the grave after the ghost disappeared inside. Tindar married Silfra and they were never again bothered by any more ghosts.

And no more is written about that.

THE THREE TROLLS OF VIK

There were once three trolls who loved the ocean. They all lived together on the southern coast of Iceland. These trolls were named Skessudrangur, Laddrangur and Langhamar. They didn't love the sound of the water, nor did they love the smell or the feel. They didn't really like how it looked in the moonlight or even how many fish there were for them to eat.

What these three loved about the ocean were all the vessels that sailed there. Big ships, Viking longboats, or small fishing crafts, the trolls knew that there were treasures to steal or things to eat on these boats. So, they made their home on the coast next to a major seafaring route and would wade out and snatch one anytime they pleased.

Their only limitation was the daytime. Like most trolls in Iceland, they would turn to stone if caught in direct sunlight. They had to be very careful because in the summertime, the sun would shine all day and most of the night. During the warmest part of the year, it was only dark for a few hours after midnight. During those summer months, they had to be ready and be very fast. Ship captains and fishermen soon learned not to sail their ships along Iceland's southern coast after dark.

There came one day, a big storm blew a ship off course. The seas were choppy and the winds were strong. The captain of the beautiful three-masted ship could not fight the current and the winds. They headed straight for the coast of Iceland.

Langhamar was on watch and spotted the ship when it was still a great distance offshore.

"Hi-Hi Ho-Ho!" He shouted excitedly to Skessudrangur and Laddrangur. They came running when he called.

They stood side by side and eagerly watched as the ship was driven closer. The ship looked bigger as it grew closer. They could soon see the crew of the ship working desperately to fight the current and avoid the coast. They fought as hard as they could, but the storm was too strong.

Laddrangur stepped into the water and motioned to the others to follow. Together, the three waded out to the ship. Laddrangur grabbed ahold of the bow at the front and Skessudrangur latched onto the center mast. They started to drag the ship towards the coastline. The sailors were ready for them. They had all known if the ship came too close to the coast, they would have to fight trolls. They had planned, practiced and had many weapons ready for battle.

When the trolls grabbed them, half of the crew rushed to the front and attacked Laddrangur's fingers with sharp spears and clubs. Other sailors shimmied up the center poles and threw spears and rocks at Skessudrangur. The rest stood with more clubs and spears, attacking each place that Langhamar tried to grab hold.

The trolls had not expected this. They always dragged the ships, with sailors or fishermen screaming or jumping into the water to swim away. None had ever fought this hard before. Each of the trolls soon had cuts and bruises on their hands and they struggled to drag the big ship closer to the shore.

The sailors fought and Langhamar let go, he grabbed again and the sailors thumped his beefy troll hands with their oars and any handy weapon. The ship caught the current and gained distance from the trolls.

Skessudrangur dove to grab the stern, latching on and digging his long fingernails into the wood. Panting, Langhamar and Laddrangur each grabbed on and all three pulled together. They dragged the ship inch by inch towards the coastline.

They didn't realize the sailors had stopped fighting. With the captain at the center, they were clustered together on the deck, smiling. In the east, the first rays of the morning sun were peeking over the horizon. They had won the battle with the trolls.

Moments later, the sun hit the trolls full on and they all turned into stone. The sailors continued on their way without any more excitement. The three trolls of stone still stand today in the water just outside the town of Vik.

THE GRIMSEY MAN AND THE POLAR BEAR

One bitterly cold winter on Grimsey, a small island north of Iceland, all the fires went out and no one could restart them. They had no tinder and no spark. It was so cold that the Grimsey Sound was frozen solid. Fortunately, there was no snow falling and the wind was calm. This was a good thing, because they could walk on the ice to the mainland and bring back fire.

The people voted and chose three of the strongest, heartiest men to make the journey. The group set out very early one morning, walking across the ice toward the mainland. They made good progress until they were about halfway across the sound. There, they came upon a crack in the ice. Turning to the right and left, it stretched as far as they could see. It did not seem too wide, and the first man thought he could jump across.

He backed up, took a running start, leapt up and over the crack, and landed safely on the other side. The other two smiled and cheered.

The second man did the same, and just as he started to jump, he slipped. His arms and legs pedaled in wide circles and he struggled desperately in the air to reach the other side. He came down close to the edge, with his feet slipping, hanging over into the empty space. He scrambled and crawled, barely pulling himself up to safety on the other side.

The third man stood still, very afraid. He didn't think now that he could make the jump. What if he fell into the crack? It was so deep, when he looked over the edge, he could not see the bottom. He shook his head, backing up from the edge.

"I can't jump that far," he shouted to the other two men.

"Go back to the village, we will bring back the fire," one of them replied.

"Safe journey, brothers," he said and watched as they continued on their way.

He felt very bad that he didn't go with them. Instead of going back to the village, he thought he would walk along the crack to see if there was a narrow place he could jump across. He walked and walked and could not find a way across. Hours later, the sky turned gray, a fierce wind started to blow, and a driving rain came. He pulled his coat up and walked into the storm. Suddenly, he heard a loud cracking sound and the ice beneath his feet broke away. He realized he was now on an iceberg, floating out to sea.

He shivered for hours as the small iceberg floated on the water. Just as he was drifting off to sleep, the small chunk of ice ran into land. He immediately jumped from the small iceberg onto the solid ground, wincing at the pain in his stiff joints. When he looked up, he saw a female polar bear lying with her cubs right in front of him. Already cold and hungry, he now feared for his life.

The mother bear saw the man and looked at him for a while. He stayed very still as he watched her get up and walk toward him. He thought surely he would end up as the polar bear's dinner. To his surprise, the bear came right up to him and sniffed. She walked around behind him and nudged him in the back with her nose. Startled, the man scrambled away. She came up to him again, pushing him again with her nose. He realized she was pushing him to where her cubs were curled up in her lair.

Very afraid, he moved slowly to where she pushed him. Once she had pushed him next to her cubs, the polar bear laid down, wrapping her warm body around him and her cubs. The man was very grateful for the warmth and soon fell asleep.

The next day, the bear got up and brought food to her cubs. She treated her human guest like one of her cubs, offering him a pile of fish. After they finished eating, he watched the mother bear. The mother bear watched him back.

After a time, she got up, walked over and pushed him. Like the night before, each time he moved she pushed him again. He understood more quickly that she was directing him. This time, she led him to the middle of the ice, where she laid down at his feet. He stood next to her until he realized she wanted him to climb on her back. He jumped astride her, but she immediately shook herself like a wet dog. At the violent shaking, he fell off and landed hard on the ice. The polar bear stared at him, then walked back to where her cubs waited. Very confused, the man followed her back to the lair.

Every day, the polar bear would have him walk with her to the middle of the ice. He would climb on her back and she would shake until he fell off. He did not understand, but did as she directed. He needed her for the warmth of her lair and the fish she supplied him to eat each day. Without those things, he would certainly die there on the ice.

On the fourth day, the man held on to her fur tightly and no matter how much the polar bear shook, he did not fall off of her back. Then, she jumped into the sea with the man on her back and swam to the island of Grimsey.

He was so happy to have made it home, he walked the polar bear straight through town to his farm. He gave her as much milk as she wanted to drink and two fat sheep for her cubs. She accepted his gifts, and calmly returned to the sea.

As she swam back to her cubs, the astonished townsfolk all stood watching. As the polar bear disappeared from sight, a ship appeared on the horizon. They knew the other men had made it to the mainland and were returning with the fire and all cheered.

THE STONE BOAT

There was once a powerful Chieftain who had a son named Sigurd.
Sigurd was a strong, handsome man who was accomplished in the
Viking ways. One day, the Chieftain told Sigurd it was time to find a
wife. The Chieftain wanted to hand over leadership of the people,
but it was tradition for the leaders to be a married couple. For Sigurd
to lead, he must have a wife that would be able to help him with the
tasks necessary to lead the tribe.

Sigurd was lonely and wanted to get married so he was happy to
do as his father wished. Sigurd knew all the women of the village but
none suited him. He packed a bag and set sail in his longboat to find
his bride. As he traveled, he visited friends he had made during his
previous travel. He talked to each one and asked for introductions to
find just the right girl to marry. In this way, he came to know of a
princess everyone said was wise, beautiful and kind. Sigurd was
anxious to meet this girl and immediately set out for the kingdom.

When he arrived at the land far from his home, Sigurd met the
princess named Annika. He fell in love with her beauty and charm
and she, in turn, fell in love with him. He wasted no time in asking
her father, the king, for her hand in marriage.

Annika's father was old and sick and knew he would not live
much longer. He agreed to allow Sigurd to marry Annika but only if
Sigurd agreed to stay in their kingdom to rule the land. He missed
his own family and his home, but he loved Annika. Sigurd sent a
message to his father that he would stay in Annika's kingdom until
Annika's younger brother was old enough to rule. Then, they could
return to Iceland and lead the tribe.

Sigurd and Annika were married and lived happily for several years in Annika's homeland. One day, the sad news came that Sigurd's father had died. Sigurd immediately made plans to return home. He and Annika packed up their belongings, and with their young son, Silvu, they boarded a ship and started the three-day journey to Iceland.

After two days, an odd calm came over the sea. The winds stopped and the water was still. Princess Annika was on the deck of the ship with Silvu while Sigurd and the crew were sleeping below. As she looked out over the calm water, she saw something in the water and realized it was a small craft. As it came alongside the ship, Annika saw it was an odd-looking stone boat. The only person in the boat was a horribly ugly witch. Annika was so afraid, she could not speak. She found her voice was frozen and could not cry out to the sailors or Sigurd for help.

The evil witch climbed aboard the ship and grabbed little Silvu from his mother. She snatched Annika's silk robe and ripped the gold ribbons from her hair. Moving quickly, the witch put on the clothes she had stolen. As Annika watched, the ugly witch transformed into a human being. Even more surprising, the witch now looked exactly like Annika. The witch then threw Annika into the stone boat and spoke in a dreadful voice.

"Go, boat! Do not slow or change course until you arrive in the kingdom of the underworld."

Annika held on as the boat flew away and was soon far from the big ship. When the stone boat was gone, Silvu started to cry. The witch rocked and sang, but no matter what she tried, she could not calm him. In desperation, she woke Sigurd, yelling at him for leaving her alone with a crying child while he enjoyed a peaceful sleep.

"How thoughtless, husband, to leave me alone to watch our child and the ship too! I cannot possibly take care of so many things. Come up here right now and help me," she cried.

Sigurd was surprised to hear his wife yelling. He had never heard her raise her voice, or say a harsh word to anyone. He didn't stop to think on this too much, because Silvu was still crying. He took his son and tended to him. He baby wouldn't sleep or eat. Sigurd offered toys, brought out sweets and milk but nothing would stop Silvu's crying. Sigurd spent the rest of the trip tending to his son. Fortunately, a good breeze blew and the sailors were able to hoist the sails. They made the rest of the trip in a very short time.

When they reached their new home, Sigurd found the people were sad and missed the old Chieftain but were very happy Sigurd returned home. They were all pleased by his wife and child, but wondered why the young boy cried all the time. From the time they came off the ship, poor Silvu never stopped crying. He had always been such a good child, so Sigurd arranged for a nurse to stay with him. As soon as the nurse took over his care, he stopped crying and was a happy little boy again.

Sigurd noticed that since they arrived, Annika was also very different. He did not like the change. She had become stubborn and difficult, and now had a mean streak and arrogance she never had before. She kept to herself, and even at mealtimes spoke very little and ate even less. Many people noticed her short temper and she had few friends in the court. Most people went out of their way to avoid her.

One day there were two young men playing chess in the sitting room next to Annika's. They thought it was odd when they heard her talking but never saw anyone enter or leave the room. Curious, the next day, they moved their game closer to the door, to better eavesdrop. One was more daring and looked through a crack in the door.

In shock, he pulled his friend over to watch with him. They both watched as Annika stood in front of the mirror.

"When I yawn a little, then I am a pretty human woman; when I yawn half-way, my witch nature shows half-way; and when I yawn all the way, then I am my beautiful witch self all the way."

As she said this, she gave a huge yawn and instantly turned into a hideous ugly witch. Just then, a deep hole opened up in the floor and a massive three-headed giant appeared. He pulled an enormous bowl of meat through the hole and set it before her. As the two boys watched, she bent her head down, looking more like a troll as she snarled and snorted. With slobber and spit flying, she ate until the bowl was empty.

As soon as she was finished, the three-headed giant took the bowl and disappeared. As the hole in the floor closed, Annika resumed her human form. The boys ran away frightened. They knew no one would ever believe their story about the horrible troll-witch Annika really was.

At that same moment, on the other side of the large castle, Silvu sat on his nurse's lap as she read him a bedtime story. With a loud crack and groaning of wood, several planks of the wood floor flew up and a large hole appeared. The nurse watched as a beautiful woman, who looked a lot like Annika, dressed in white, walked toward them. She had a metal ring around her waist and it was connected to a heavy iron chain that went down into the hole.

Without a word, the woman came up to the nurse, gently picked up Silvu and gave him a long hug. Tears in her eyes, she returned him to the nurse's lap and slowly walked back into the hole in the floor. The nurse was certain this was a ghost or spirit and told no one about the visit. The next night, the woman visited again, and again was silent as she hugged Silvu.

As she was leaving, the nurse heard the spirit say, "Two are gone, and one only is left."

The nurse was afraid now that the child was in danger. She thought the woman was sad but did not seem dangerous, but she decided to tell the boy's father. The next morning, she went to Sigurd and told him the whole story. She asked if he would be in the nursery that night when the spirit came to visit. Sigurd agreed, and that night stood ready with his sword drawn.

When the floorboards flew up, he saw the mysterious woman in white chained just as the nurse had described. He immediately recognized her as his beloved Annika. He swung his sword and with a deafening crash, he spit the iron chain in two. The entire castle rumbled and shook and everyone for miles heard an awful groaning and shrieking. The chain fell back into the hole, and the floor closed up.

The real Annika stood before him and told him the entire story. The horrible troll-witch had cast a spell and took her place up here, while Annika had been chained in the underworld. The three-headed giant was her jailor. He had fallen in love with her and wanted to marry her, but she refused. Finally, she had come up with a plan to escape. She told the giant she would marry him if she could visit her son for three nights in a row. He agreed, but to make sure she didn't

escape, he put the chain around her waist. When Sigurd cut through the chain, the thunderous sound was the giant falling back down the tunnel to the underworld.

The witch's spell was broken and everyone saw her for the troll she really was and they chased her into the mountains where she fell off a cliff and was buried in a landslide.

TALE OF A RAVEN

In the North of Iceland, there is a valley called Vatnsdalur (vat-ness-dalur), which means "Lake Valley". There are mountain on all sides, with steep slopes. A long time ago, there was a farm called Gullberastadir (good-bear-a-sta-there) in this valley that was home to a servant girl named Edel.

Edel worked in the house, cleaning the floors, baking bread and cooking dinners, and washing the family's clothes. She stayed busy from sunrise until sunset each day. Even though she worked hard and was often tired, she always took time for the animals. She would walk down by the barn to greet the cows and laugh at the playful goats jumping over each other and the blocks of hay. She would wander further to pet the horses and share small cubes of sugar with them.

She was fond of all the animals on the farm, but loved the birds most of all. Every day, she would take time from her household chores to sit and visit with the animals. When it was time for lunch, Edel would take her bread and cheese outside and sit on the grass in front of the house. As she ate her picnic lunch, birds would often land nearby for crumbs. There was a sleek black raven with bright eyes that came every day. Edel would save the biggest crumbs for her raven friend.

One day, Edel tossed a morsel of food in front of the raven but, to her surprise, he wouldn't eat it. She got up and picked the crumb back up, this time throwing it a little further away. Still, the raven would not accept it. Edel was concerned her feathered friend was sick or injured. He didn't look sick and as she watched him fly, he didn't seem to be hurt. As she watched, Edel was relieved when the raven flew close and landed at her feet. She bent down and put another crumb on the ground.

The raven ignored the food and hopped away, then stopped and looked back. Edel thought the bird wanted her to follow. Slowly, she got up and took a step in his direction. The raven took flight, dove down near Edel's head, then landed a few feet away and started hopping again. Edel was confused but continued to follow. Before long, she had followed the bird across the pasture and they were a long distance from the house.

As they reached the edge of the field, Edel heard a great rumbling far up in the mountains. She looked up to see where the sound came from, but it seemed to come from everywhere. As she watched, a huge cloud seemed to rise from the mountain and roll down the hillside. It came from three different directions at once.

It was a landslide of mud and rocks that rolled down the side of the mountain. As she watched, the avalanche of dirt and boulders became bigger and bigger. As it reached the bottom, Edel watched as the farmhouse disappeared, completely buried.

The raven seemed happy now, cheerfully munching on the crumbs Edel had thrown. She was saved by her feathered friend, who repaid the kindness of the food she had shared.

Since the farmhands had been in the field and the animals in the pasture, only the house itself was damaged. The farmer was so upset at the loss, he moved to the south and started a new life as a fisherman.

HELGA, AN ICELANDIC FAIRY TALE

In the early days of Iceland, there was a farmer who had three daughters. The oldest girl, Fredegone, was the apple of her mother's eye. The middle daughter, Olga was her father's favorite. Both girls were both very spoiled and vain. They spent hours arranging their hair and admiring themselves in the mirror. Their parents showered the two girls with gifts and trinkets, giving them anything they wanted.

The youngest, Helga, was made to do all the chores. She was the most beautiful of the three. She was also very kind-hearted and a hard worker. She was busy from sunrise until sunset every day. She cleaned the house, prepared the family meals and helped her father in the fields. Unlike her sisters, Helga did not receive any presents or new clothes. No one ever said thank you for all that she did. Her jealous sisters would instead give her a dirty look or a punch in the arm. She did not complain, because she had a gentle spirit and loved her family very much.

One day, while Helga was working in the field, Fredegone and Olga were dressing each other's hair. Not paying attention, they allowed the fire in the hearth to go out. In those days, there were no matches to strike and they did not have a flint stone. If the fire went out, a new fire had to be fetched. A heavy pot was used to carry hot embers that would catch fire to the wood. The farm was a great distance away from any neighbor and someone would have to fetch the embers from a cave where they knew a fire was burning. Because Helga was busy in the field, her father told Fredegone she would have to go to the cave and bring back the fire.

The day was fine and warm with bright sunshine so Fredegone thought a walk would be pleasant. Swinging the firepot as she walked, she started along the path. After she had gone a ways, as she was passing a hillock, she heard a deep voice.

"Would you rather have me with you or against you?" the voice asked.

Fredegone looked around, but didn't see who was speaking to her. She thought it was a very odd question. But then she decided didn't care in the least who was asking or why they wanted an answer. It was obviously some lowly worker that shouldn't be speaking to her. It was very rude of a stranger to even speak to her, she thought, she was obviously above them. Ignoring the question, she continued on her way to the cave.

When she arrived at the cave, she found it to be empty. There was a large fire, a big pot of stew boiling, and fresh dough laid out for baking, but there seemed to be no one home.

"Hello?" she called.

The only reply was her own echo.

"Yoo-hoo!" she tried again. There was still no response.

Fredegone thought there was no sense in this nice meal going to waste. She cut into the dough and baked a few cakes. She was not very good at baking and very careless, so all but one of the cakes were completely burned. She scooped up a large bowl of stew, taking lots of the biggest chunks of meat and sat down with the one unburned cake.

As she was enjoying her meal, a large black dog ran up to her, wagging his tail. He sat down in front of her, begging for some food. But Fredegone angrily stomped her feet and waved her hands, slapping the dog to chase him away. The dog growled, leapt at her, and bit her hand. Fredegone screamed, threw her bowl at the dog and ran out of the cave. She ran all the way home before she realized she didn't bring the fire.

She sobbed to her parents about her terrible experience. They consoled her, bandaged her hand and tucked her into bed. As sorry as they were for her injury, they were very sad she did not bring the fire back from the cave. They still needed the fire and Helga had hours more work to finish that day. Olga was their favorite and they did not want to send her to the cave, but they had no choice.

So, Olga set out on the same path that Fredegone had traveled. Like her sister, she walked by the hillock and heard a voice speaking to her.

"Would you rather have me with you or against you?" a deep voice asked.

"How dare you speak to me?" she replied angrily, "be gone with you!" She turned, stuck her nose in the air and stomped on her way.

Soon forgetting about the voice, she arrived at the cave a short time later. It was empty, just as her sister described, except for the bubbling pot of stew and the tray of dough. She had no thought of anyone else, certainly not of the person who lived in the cave or who had started to make the meal. She thought only of herself. She took the dough and made two cakes, throwing the rest of the dough into the fire. When the cakes were ready, she scooped up a large bowl of stew, taking a much of the tender potatoes and carrots as she could, and some of the best pieces of meat.

She ate until she was full, but didn't finish the bowl of stew and only pecked at one cake. As she finished her meal, the black dog came up to her, wagging his tail and begging for food. Olga reached for some boiling broth and threw it his direction. He growled and jumped at her, biting her nose clean through. Olga ran home crying, with only half a nose and no fire.

The old man and his wife were very upset for now they had two injured daughters and still no fire. Neither of them was willing to risk themselves in the cave, so they decided to send Helga. They would be most upset to lose such a good worker, but they needed the fire. Carrying the fire-pail with her, Helga followed the path to the cave.

Just as both of her sisters had done, Helga came to the hillock along the trail. And, just as her sisters had, she heard a gruff voice ask, "Would you rather I was with you than against you?"

Helga thought carefully. "A well-known proverb says, 'There is nothing so bad that it is not better to have it on your side than against you.'" She said, "I do not know who you are, but I would rather have you as a friend than an enemy."

She stood waiting for an answer, but there was only silence. She shook her head at the odd exchange, and continued down the path until she came to the cave. As she entered, it was just as both her sisters described. The stew was bubbling, and a fresh tray of dough stood ready, but the cave was deserted. Helga stirred the pot and prepared the dough into cakes and set them to bake. She was very hungry, because her only breakfast was dry bread and water.

Her parents had not sent any food with her for lunch and now her stomach was growling loudly. The stew smelled very good, but she did not want to take any without asking permission. Having nothing else to do, and being very tired from her walk, Helga sat down to wait for the owner of the cave.

No sooner had she sat down when she felt a violent shaking and a tremendous rumbling sound. It seemed that the entire cave might come down on her head and she stood up, ready to run outside. Just then, the cave entrance was blocked by a hideous three-headed giant and a huge, fierce-looking black dog. Helga was very afraid, but she loved animals and carefully held out her hand to the dog. He immediately wagged his tail and ran over to her that she could scratch his ears.

The giant looked around and nodded. "You did well to complete the work you saw needed to be done. I thank you."

Helga was pleased at the compliment as he continued, "I would like to share my meal with you and then provide the fire you need to take home."

Helga wondered how he knew of her errand, but did not ask any questions.

The giant reached over to the shelf and took down two bowls. He filled one for Helga, which he handed to her, and then filled a bowl for himself. As she accepted the bowl, the ground began to shake, like an earthquake, and she heard a thunderous noise, booming and crashing. Helga was very afraid.

The giant spoke in a peaceful and gentle voice, "Sit here beside me and we will eat."

He did not seem concerned about the disturbance around them, and calmly handed her a cake, and this made Helga feel much better. She ate the stew and cake but as soon as she finished, the uproar started again. The ground shook, thunder boomed and lightning streaked through the sky, hitting the entrance to the cave.

Helga was so terrified by the sudden storm that she ran up to the giant, jumping beside him and buried her face in his arm. The storm passed and she looked up, embarrassed, but saw there was no

longer an ugly giant next to her. She held the arm of a handsome young man. She pulled away, confused.

"Do not be afraid, Helga" he said. "My name is Torkell. Many people who have come here are selfish or afraid. Your kindness and acceptance has rescued me from the curse of living as a three-headed giant. I thank you."

"How did this happen?" she asked, worried she might turn into the monster next.

"My father was to be King in our land and he spurned the affection of a powerful wicked fairy named Gondomar who wanted to be Queen. He chose instead to marry my mother. When I was born, as revenge, Gondomar cursed me with an enchantment that changed me into the horrible beast you saw. Only someone who could look past that and trust me completely would break the curse."

"I am happy I could help you, Prince Torkell." She said, "But I have been gone from my home for a very long time and my parents will be quite angry I have taken so long." She told him of her sisters and the work she was expected to do at home. She was very worried if she did not return with the fire soon, her parents would scold and punish her.

"I do not like that you must go back there, but I will give you protection until I come back," he said. "I must return to my parents and let them know the curse is broken, then I will come back for you."

Torkell went to the back of the cave and unearthed a small chest that he brought and handed to Helga. "This is filled with gold and precious jewels that you can share with your family. But this," he said unfolding a light tunic of pure gold, "you must wear under your clothes and take care that no one sees it. It is woven with magic and will protect you."

Helga cried and thanked him for the generous gifts. She put on the gold dress, carefully covered it with her old threadbare one and put the jewels in a sack to carry home. Torkell filled the fire-shovel with burning coals, and they started down the path to Helga's home, walking together. Torkell had carried the shovel for her, but they stopped when they were within sight of the cottage. Giving her a warm hug, he put a heavy gold ring on her finger.

"Keep this ring, Helga, and do not let anyone take it from you. The ring is my promise that I will return to you," he said, "I will be back as soon as I can."

When Helga reached the cottage, her mother and father were very glad to see her. They hugged her and praised her for doing a good job. Her parents and both sisters thanked her for the fire, but soon forgot all about it when she showed them the sack she had brought with her.

Fredegone and Olga grabbed it and pounced on the jewels as they spilled out. They each grabbed as much as they could, dividing the precious stones between them, leaving the empty bag for Helga. She did not complain, for she had hidden the dress and the gold ring Torkell had given her and both were safe.

The happiness at home didn't last and soon things were back to the way they had always been. Fredegone and Olga did nothing all day but sit around the house admiring themselves, arranging their hair and playing with their new jewels. Helga was left to do all the housework and help in the fields. This went on for nearly a week.

One day, they saw a big beautiful ship lying anchored in the harbor. Helga's father ran to the beach to greet the crew. On the beach, he met the captain, who was a handsome young man and they struck up a conversation. The old man asked many clever questions, but could not get the young man to share his name. The young man posed many questions to the old man about his family and children.

"I have two daughters," the old man said proudly, "and they are both such good and beautiful girls."

"If you're agreeable, I should like very much to meet them," said the young captain.

The old man was overjoyed and quickly showed the young man to the house. Fredegone and Olga had hurried to put on their best dresses and draped themselves with many of the jewels they had taken from Helga.

After meeting each girl and talking with them, the young captain took the farmer aside to speak privately.

"Your daughters seem pleasant, but what has happened to them? One had a bandaged hand and the other a bandana across her nose," he said.

The farmer waved his hand and mumbled about an accident on the cliff. He soon saw the captain did not believe his story. Afraid the captain would leave, he admitted the truth. He shared the story of the strange cave and the vicious dog attack.

The sea captain listened to the story intently until the farmer stopped talking.

"So, how did you get the fire, then? Did you have another daughter to send? Perhaps one that is patient and kind to animals."

"No!" the farmer insisted too quickly. "I mean, well, yes, I do have another daughter but she is not like the others."

Looking around, he said, "She is ugly, lazy, and bad-tempered. I did not want you to meet her and think badly of the rest of the family."

The young captain insisted, so the farmer had no choice but to call to Helga.

When she appeared in her threadbare dress and dirt-smeared face, the captain smiled. He went up to her and as he held out his hand, her shabby dress fell away, revealing the beautiful gold gown he had given her. Her sisters stood by, gaping in surprise and furious.

Prince Torkell told Helga's parents he would be marrying her and scolded the whole family for their terrible treatment of her. Instead of being allowed to keep all the jewels he had sent, each family member could choose only one. Prince Torkell and Helga boarded his ship and sailed off to his home, where they were married and lived the rest of their days together.

ASUMUND & SIGNY

In the early days of Iceland, there was a time when trolls caused great problems. They were constantly up to no good. When they wanted a snack, they would steal sheep from the flocks grazing in the high pastures. They would throw rocks to keep travelers from using the mountain passes. Others stayed along the coast and would sink boats to keep the settlers from catching fish in the fjords and surrounding ocean. The problem became so bad that many warriors came from other lands to help fight the trolls.

One of these lands was home to a Prince named Asmund and his sister, Princess Signy. Their father, the King, had gone to Iceland to fight the trolls. While the King was gone, Prince Asmund ruled the land and watched over his sister. Princess Signy was beautiful and kind. She had many suitors but had not chosen one as a husband. Knights and princes from other lands came to meet her to win her heart but none had succeeded yet.

One day, they received word that Prince Ring was on his way from a neighboring kingdom to meet Princess Signy. Prince Ring had heard of Signy's beauty and was determined to marry her. She had heard of his bravery and knew he was handsome so she was looking forward to meeting him as well.

Along the way, Prince Ring traveled a narrow trail through a dense forest. There were large beautiful trees providing lots of shade and the ride was uneventful. Around midday, he came to a clearing where he decided to stop for a meal. As he sat, he heard a voice singing. He looked around and saw a beautiful woman picking flowers nearby. A small basket sat at her feet.

"Hello there," he said, approaching her, "Why are you here alone? Do you need any help?"

"Oh my, no, I was just picking flowers," she answered quickly, "I live nearby. I don't think I've ever seen you before."

"I am Prince Ring," he answered with a bow, "I have come to meet the Princess Signy."

"Oh, but I am Princess Signy," said the girl with a wave of her hand.

Prince Ring bowed to her, lightly kissing the hand she offered. "I am quite pleased to meet you Princess Signy. You are as beautiful as I have heard."

She thanked him and blushed.

"Would you share a meal with me?" he asked.

"Only if I can share this terta I have with you," she answered, showing him the sweet cake from the basket.

They sat together and shared his hearty meal of bread and cheese. She insisted he then share the terta cake she had brought. Prince Ring had no way of knowing the creature he dined with was actually a troll-witch, disguised by powerful magic to look beautiful to Prince Ring. The terta was laced with more magic that would ensure the spell bound him for a very long time.

By the time the meal was finished, Prince Ring begged the troll-witch to come away with him to his home and marry him. She still pretended to be Princess Signy and returned home with him.

As Prince Ring made plans for a wedding and celebration, the troll-witch made plans for an invasion to take over his kingdom. She sent secret messages to her family of trolls and giants so they could prepare. The troll-witch planned an attack during the wedding ceremony when everyone would be distracted.

Several weeks passed and Prince Ring continued to be distracted by his soon-to-be bride. He did not notice the signs of trolls in the area. Sheep were missing. Unexplained avalanches of rocks in the mountains. Nearby, Prince Asmund received word there were trolls in the area of his home.

He led a patrol along the border of Prince Ring's kingdom. His well-trained knights quickly found the trolls' camp and surrounded them. Before capturing them, Prince Asmund overheard the trolls' plan to attack Prince Ring and Princess Signy's wedding.

Prince Asmund immediately sent his most trusted knight on his fastest horse to Prince Ring with an urgent message. A wise wizard at Prince Ring's court concocted a powerful counter-potion to remove the curse. Once her true form was revealed, they trapped the troll-witch and imprisoned her.

Prince Ring and his sister traveled to Prince Asmund's court to thank them for the warning that saved the kingdom. There, he finally met the real Princess Signy. Ring fell in love with Signy at first sight, and Asmund with Ring's sister, so they had a double wedding. Ring and Asmund each ruled their kingdoms and from then on never had any more trouble with trolls.

GILITRUTT

There was once a successful farmer named Leifur who lived below the mountain called Eyjafjöll (aye-ya-fee-yolt) in the South of Iceland. He worked hard, spending long hours tending to his land and animals. He had good pastures for his large herd of sheep. He felt he was ready to marry and chose a beautiful girl named Dara from a nearby village as his bride. Soon after they were married, he found out Dara was very lazy. She had no interest in the work of a farmer's wife. She did no milking, or collecting eggs from the chickens. She didn't even like to clean the house. Leifur was disappointed but discovered there was not much he could do to get his wife to work.

One of the jobs that every farmer's wife was expected to do was to weave wool into cloth. In the fall, he gave her a large bag of wool and asked her to work it into cloth, but Dara mumbled an excuse and generally ignored the request. By the onset of winter, she hadn't touched the wool, even though Leifur often asked her about the progress. She became frustrated, knowing she had to make the cloth but she desperately wanted to find a way to avoid the task. Working wool into cloth was very time consuming and difficult work, she thought. They would need the cloth for clothes, but she so didn't want to have to make it.

One day, as she lay napping in front of the house, a very large, ugly and wrinkled old woman came to her and asked her for food. Even though she was lazy, she was very smart and a quick thinker.

"I will provide you food, but would you be willing to work?" asked Dara.

"Perhaps, if I'm able," said the old woman. "What task do you need done?"

"I have a large amount of wool that must be worked into cloth," Dara replied.

"Yes, yes," answered the old woman, "bring me what you have."

Dara gave the large sack of wool to the old woman, along with a big sack of bread, cheese and dried meat. The old woman took both bundles, slung them on her back, and said, "I'll return with the cloth on the first day of summer."

"How much will you charge me? Will you require cash or barter in food?" Dara asked.

"No, this food now is enough pay for me," said the crone.

"No, no, that is such a large amount of wool to work. I must pay you more, surely there is something I have you want."

The old crone smiled craftily. "In exchange for the work, you must tell me my name. I will give you three guesses and if you get it right, you owe me nothing more."

Dara thought this a very odd and silly request so she quickly agreed to the terms, and the old woman left.

As the winter passed, Leifur often asked his wife about her progress on the wool. She would smile and tell him not to worry, that the cloth would be ready on the first day of summer. He was not pleased with the answer. He never saw Dara working on any cloth, and although he searched everywhere, he could not find the bag of wool. But, he didn't want to argue with her so he did not ask about the missing wool.

Late in winter, Dara began to ponder over the old woman's name. She wondered about the strange request and realized it may not have been as silly as she thought. If the old woman were a troll or ogre, the outcome could be quite bad. The more she thought about it the more afraid she became. When she realized she had no way of finding out the old woman's name, she became very worried and depressed about it.

Leifur saw how upset she became, and asked her to tell him what was wrong. She admitted her deception and told him the whole story about the old woman. Leifur was very afraid for Dara. He had no doubt the old woman was a troll who intended to abduct her when she couldn't supply the name.

Several days later, while tending his sheep, Leifur found himself in foothills of the mountains. He stopped to rest at a large rocky mound, and was soon deep in thought about how to help his wife

with her problem. He heard a thumping sound coming from inside the mound. He jumped up, away from the mound, surprised. He walked closer to investigate the strange sound. To his amazement, he came upon a crack in the mound and through it he saw a huge woman sitting at a loom.

She held the loom between her knees and as she beat the web, he could hear her chanting.

> "Hi and ho!
> The silly wife doesn't know my name
> Hi hi and ho ho!
> Gilitrutt is my name ho ho!!
> Gilitrutt is my name
> Hi hi and ho ho!"

She hummed happily to herself, as she worked with great energy. The farmer was giddy with happiness. He was sure that this strange troll was the same old woman who had made the bargain with his wife. He went straight home and wrote the name down on a piece of paper: Gilitrutt. He kept the name a secret and did not share the story with Dara.

The last day of winter arrived, and Dara was very afraid for the old woman's arrival the next day. She was so upset she could think of nothing else and went back to bed, burying herself in the pillows and blankets. Her husband came to her and asked if she knew the name of the old woman. She said she did not and moaned that her life was surely over.

"You will soon be mourning me, my husband," she groaned, flopping back on the bed and pulling the covers back over her head.

"I doubt that," Leifur said with a smile. He handed her the piece of paper with the name on it, then told her what he had seen at the rocky mound.

Dara laughed as she danced around the room, and hugged him tightly. She took the paper but asked if he would spend the day with her, just in case the name was wrong.

"No," he said. "Your laziness put you in this danger. You made the deal by yourself now you must pay her by yourself." He left to move the sheep to another pasture, telling her he would be back in a few days.

The next day was the first day of summer. Dara lay alone in her bed, too afraid to rise and face the day. All too soon, she heard a booming, rumbling noise. She jumped out of bed just as the old woman pulled open the door and stepped inside. Even in the dim light, the farmer's wife could see how disfigured and ugly the old woman was.

She flung down a huge roll of cloth, saying, "The cloth is made. I have kept my end of our bargain and now you must as well. What is my name?"

Dara, nearly frightened to death, stammered, "Signy?"

"That's my name? That's my name? No, guess again, missy," said the old woman.

"Asa?" questioned Dara.

"That's my name? That's my name?" the crone crowed. "Ha! Last guess, mistress!"

"Maybe its Gilitrutt!" shouted Dara.

The old troll had such a shock that she fell headlong on the floor, making a thunderous noise. She jumped back up and ran out the door, never to be seen again.

As for Dara, she was so grateful to have been delivered from this troll that she became a different person. From that time on, she was known to work as hard as her husband. She became an excellent housekeeper and always worked her wool herself.

HABOGI

In Iceland's former days, there were three sisters who lived with their parents. All three were old enough to be married, but none had chosen a husband. Their parents feared none would ever get married. The father, losing his patience, told each girl to choose the first name of their future husbands.

The oldest decided she wanted her husband to have the name Sigmund. It was a common name and it narrowed her choices, but it still left her with a lot of men to choose from. The second daughter chose the name Siguard. She knew of at least seven men in the village with that name, and she quite liked several of them. She felt she could choose one of the Siguards as a husband and be quite happy.

"Good, this is good," her father said, "Now, Helga, what name is your choice?"

She heard a whisper in her ear, and thinking it must be the Hidden People helping her, she answered without hesitation.

"Habogi."

"Habogi?" This surprised her entire family. None of them had ever heard of anyone named Habogi.

Helga insisted that was to be the name of her future husband and no amount of talking from her parents could change her mind. So, their father told everyone that the girls had chosen the names of their future husbands.

Those with the chosen names were asked to come court each of the sisters.

For weeks after, every man with the name Sigmund or Sigurd from all around the area came to court the older sisters. A few men

came to call on Helga, but none were named Habogi. She watched as her sisters entertained and held parties. Helga would attend, but always be alone. She was not unhappy, she was certain Habogi would come for her.

In time, each of the older sisters selected men and chose a date for a double wedding. They begged Helga to choose a different name for her husband so that she too could marry.

She replied, "No, Habogi will come for me. I will wait."

The day of her sisters' wedding came and preparations were made for a great party. Many people from far and wide came to help celebrate the marriages. In the middle of the festivities, a dirty old peasant came to the house and asked for Helga. She came and greeted him politely, trying not to get too close as he seemed dirty and did not smell pleasant.

"I am Habogi," he said. "I have come to take you away to marry me."

Helga looked into his eyes and smiled. "I will go with you."

Her parents protested and worried that such an old and obviously poor man would not be able to take care of their daughter. Helga wouldn't listen to their objections. She waved her hand and said she was certain everything would be fine. She enjoyed the rest of the day with her family at the weddings.

The next morning, the old man returned with a beautiful horse, wearing a fine saddle trimmed in red and gold. He helped Helga on the horse. They said goodbye to her family and started on their way to Habogi's home.

They rode past a big meadow with a large herd of sheep.

He pointed them out and said, "The herd belongs to me, except the most beautiful one, there, the one with golden bells on its horns. That one is yours."

They rode on a little further when they came across a herd of cattle.

He pointed them out and said, "The herd also belongs to me, except one. Choose the best one and that one is yours."

Helga was surprised and pleased at his generosity. A little further on, they came to a beautiful herd of horses. Habogi told Helga this herd was also his, and she should choose whichever one she wanted to be hers.

Finally, they arrived at his home. Helga was surprised to see it was a small and shabby house. He had shown her so much on their ride, the many animals and large herds that she had expected a home more suited to a successful man.

He is such a kind and generous man, she thought, *that is much more important than a fine house.*

"Have faith," she heard a voice whisper. Again, she thought the Hidden People were encouraging her so she trusted them.

Not wanting to hurt Habogi's feeling, Helga said nothing about the house. She was thankful she had held her tongue, because once inside, she found it was beautifully furnished. He had many fine things and Helga knew she would be quite comfortable here.

After showing her around her new home, Habogi said he had many tasks to finish to prepare for the wedding. They were to be married in three days, and she would return then with her family for the festivities. He hugged her warmly and set her on the beautiful horse. He sent his brother to escort her home and keep her safe.

Once back home, Helga packed her things. After the three days, she traveled with her parents and her sisters back to Habogi's home for her wedding. They rode a group of fine horses that Habogi had sent for them and more horses carried the supplies for their stay and Helga's possessions.

As they passed the fields and pastures, Helga pointed out the herds that belonged to Habogi. Her sisters became very jealous. It seemed Helga's future husband was far wealthier than the men they had chosen. They thought it was very unfair that she had found such a man to marry. How could he have such wealth when he had looked so poor and dirty when they first met?

When they arrived at the house, the older sisters looked at each other and smirked. Helga's future husband may not be so well off if this was the house Helga was expected to live in. Their first impression that he was poor had been right, they thought. His clothes were ragged and his home small and in disrepair. It would seem Helga was not marrying very well after all.

They felt smug until they entered the little house. The furnishings were high quality and very beautiful. The rooms were comfortable and welcoming and everyone felt very much at home. As soon as they arrived, a young girl met them and showed them to rooms where each of them would be staying. She looked after their comfort and made sure they had everything they needed.

Once settled, they came to Helga's room and saw her wedding dress. It was simple and beautiful, made from a fine delicate cloth edged with gold and silver thread. The veil was folded and placed nearby. The oldest sister shook it out and saw the garment was hand-made lace with a beautiful detail. This was far finer than either of their wedding dresses had been. Helga's sisters were green with envy. Helga laughed, hugged each one and assured them they had married well and would be very happy. There was no need for their envy.

Still jealous over Helga's good fortune, the sisters each went to bed resentful and woke up bitter. Together, they snuck into Helga's room when everyone was at breakfast. They scooped ash and embers from the fireplace, intending to destroy Helga's wedding dress. Just as they turned to throw the shovelful towards the dress, Habogi appeared in front of them.

"You are Helga's sisters who she has loved dearly for years. Why are you now so envious of her happiness?" he asked. "She has wished you the best and you should do the same for her now."

They realized their pettiness and were ashamed. They each had wonderful husbands and they had no need for anything. They begged Habogi not to tell Helga of what they tried to do and Habogi agreed to keep their secret. It was never spoken of again, but the older sister always had trouble keeping her skirts from being singed in the fire when she cooked. The middle sister always had to have help lighting a fire because any she started on her own immediately went out.

Habogi and Helga had a beautiful wedding with no further interruption and Helga was quite happy. The next morning, she was shocked to find the little cottage was a palace and her dear Habogi was a handsome young prince. Her acceptance of him and the life he offered when she married him released him from an evil enchantment. They lived well and we know this is true because nothing more is written about them.

ICELANDIC PRONUNCIATION GUIDE

Áá	say like	ouch - how
Ðð	say like	this - the
Éé	say like	yet - yell
Íí	say like	eek - eel
Óó	say like	over - no
Úú	say like	loot - moot
Þþ	say like	thing - thorn
Ææ	say like	I - Ice
Öö	say like	hurry — hurt

ABOUT THE AUTHOR

Heidi Herman is a native of Illinois with a proud Scandinavian heritage. Having an Icelandic mother, she grew up with stories of brave fishermen, mischievous trolls and adventurous Vikings. After a career in telecom consulting, Heidi was inspired by her mother's memoirs, and began writing, once again being immersed in the childhood fascination of legend, lore and imaginative stories. She turned her focus to fiction writing, researching and modernizing Icelandic folk tales and stories from the Sagas.

She currently lives in Illinois with her two Schoodles, Dusty and Thor. She spends much of her time researching and writing about Iceland, having several novels and more children's stories in development. She partners with her Icelandic mother to give presentations on Iceland, attends Scandinavian events, and pursues adventure all along the way.

Other books by Heidi Herman:

Legend of the Icelandic Yule Lads

Icelandic Yule Lads & Other Legends Coloring Book

Homestyle Icelandic Cooking for American Kitchens

Made in the USA
San Bernardino, CA
28 October 2016